bodo

bodo

John Bennett

QUARTET BOOKS

First published in Great Britain by Quartet Books Ltd in 1996
A member of the Namara Group
27 Goodge Street
London W1P 2LD

First published in the U.S.A. by The Smith

A catalogue reference for this book is available from the British Library

ISBN 0 07043 8034 X

Printed and bound in Great Britain by Staples Printers Rochester Ltd,
Medway City Estate, Frindsbury, Rochester, Kent ME2 4LT.

bodo

To Pete, wherever he may be.

I: The War

Walter Steiner's German ancestors had come to Texas in the late 1840s, fleeing persecution from the Diet of the German Confederation. But by the time Walter came on the scene, his German blood had been thinned considerably, and he had to learn the language from scratch for his position in the Civil Affairs Division in occupied Germany.

Walter first heard about the CAD in the spring of 1944 at the radio station in his hometown of Beaumont. He was a radio engineer, and he was watching the announcer in the control booth through the soundproof glass while listening to him over a radio at his side. He did this often, fascinated by the disparity between the authority of the voice coming to him over the radio and the familiarity of Bugsy Carter's flushed face on the far side of the glass, a face that every Friday evening grew word-slur drunk by closing time down at the Lone Star Tavern. But when Walter heard Bugsy's voice over the radio, he believed in it, and that voice was now telling him to join the CAD.

Bugsy's voice alone would not have been enough to convince Walter to join — he wasn't so easily influenced. He was nearly thirty-five years old, single, and living with his parents. He had a mind of his own. But lately a soft melancholy had settled over Walter's days, and at times this melancholy approached the pitch of restlessness. He blamed it on the war. All his life he had functioned comfortably and obscurely on the fringes of society, and now the war was flushing him out. He wasn't physically fit to fight, but the CAD was a horse of a different color. Somewhere along the line, as the battles raged around the globe, it became clear that when the war was finally over, a large portion of civilization would lie in ashes, and an array of provisional governments would be necessary to supervise reconstruction, an array of governors-in-waiting, the CAD.

Walter was put through eight weeks of training, commissioned a captain in the army, and transported by ship to Shrivenham, England, along with five hundred other newly commissioned officers ranging in age from thirty-five to sixty. When they got off the ship in England, they hiked two hours through drizzle and mud to their billets where they slept sixteen in a room and went to chow with their mess gear clanging from their belts.

They underwent further training and waited for the war to end, and gradually the thick sadness of no-purpose settled over the camp: by the time the assignments came down, the men at Shrivenham had become seasoned cynics, hardened psychological veterans ready to match their cunning against that of orphans and displaced persons.

Walter was assigned to the German Youth Activities and rode into Munich with the Third Infantry Division. As an officer in the GYA, he worked hand-in-hand with the *Jugendamt*, a social-services tendril of the new German government that dealt mainly in war orphans.

It was no easy task, weeding out the orphans from the two million Allied fighting men and the hordes of displaced Russians, Poles, Greeks, and Rumanians who were swarming over western Germany. German citizens were caught up in this maelstrom and left wandering the countryside and city streets looking for a way of life, many of them finding it in a barter system in which a Leicha camera was worth a month's supply of coffee, Dresden china could be converted into Lucky Strikes, and children traded shy smiles for candy. It was part of the GYA's job to get hold of these children before they became incorrigible and too world-wise to handle.

And so the children were collected and stuck away in orphanages, nunneries and monasteries. Someone had to sit them down and explain away the horror, try to make light of their trembling, headaches, indigestion and anorexia, try to stop them from running from the playing fields with their hands clamped over their ears screaming *Terrorfliegen!* every time a cargo plane flew overhead; show them that the future was theirs.

* * *

Alma was a clumsy, big-boned girl who as a child was ridiculed by other children. She was clumsy and big-boned and by the age of twelve big-breasted so that boys three or four years older than she would waylay her on her way home from school, tug her down an embankment, across a field, a little ways into a forest, and in a droll, palsy way, molest her. Violate her so that the shock of it drew Alma out of her body and her spirit hovered almost clinically over the action, more with the boys than with her own body. Alma likes it, the boys said, Alma is a nymph and can't get enough, Alma is a whore, look how she lays back and takes it in.

Alma's body was not beautiful, but her breasts were large and Alma was young and reticent and the combination sent out signals. The signals were there, yes, but Alma didn't *send* them. They went out against her will, but no one privy to Alma's fate had the sensitivity to understand this, and by the time the other girls caught up with Alma physically and the boys lost interest in her, she had been driven so far into herself or so far out that her body had become a *thing* with neutered emotions. She learned to play violin mechanically, acquired clerical skills, and developed an obsession for order and predictability that at the age of thirty landed her a secretarial position in Hitler's Ministry of Propaganda.

Alma's inner life was untouched by the war until the bombs began to fall. The Munich branch of the Ministry was reduced to rubble, and a direct hit on Alma's home took the lives of her father and her two younger sisters, leaving Alma alone with her infirm mother in the remains of their home.

Each night the news coming over the crystal set told Alma that Germany was winning the war, but Alma knew better. Everyone knew better once the bombs began to fall. Alma knew that the Americans were on their way and that they would be angry. They'd be angry and out of control and they'd pillage and rape. Rape. The bombs fell and Alma trembled. She became violently ill, retching the dry heaves in a corner of the cellar, not understanding the emotions that had been spring-loaded and left in her subconscious years ago.

Alma's mother sat against the cold stone wall with a blanket wrapped around her damaged legs. She cocked her head and listened: no planes in the night sky. Some fear juice squirted into the old lady's veins, and her eyes narrowed. Her mind raced. Her daughter was cracking up right here in this dark, ugly cellar. Her daughter was cracking up and would become befuddled, the old lady had seen it. Scores of them wandering the streets, their eyes glazed and vacant. Alma would go up out of the cellar and join them, leaving her mother to die.

"Alma!" the old woman called in a sharp voice. "What is the matter with you? Get control of yourself! What would your father think! Would he be proud? No! He would be disgraced! Do you hear?"

"Oh, *Mutti, Mutti,*" Alma moaned. "Don't let them touch me, please don't. . . ."

Ah, so that was it. "Come here," the old woman crooned, her arms outstretched in the dark cellar. "Come to *Mutti*. . . ."

* * *

In July of 1945 Dwight David Eisenhower spoke to the troops in the European Theater over the newly established Armed Forces Radio. Walter sat in his BOQ room on a straight-back chair and listened. It was like old times. It was like listening to Bugsy Carter read the news over the radio while driving home from work. The news today was that the non-fraternization regulations were being rescinded. Walter listened to the entire broadcast and then sat quietly contemplating the significance of what Ike had said. He got up from his chair and went into the bathroom. He lathered up and began to shave.

The doctrine of non-fraternization was outlined in *The Soldier's Pocket Guide to Germany:* it had been decided that no one would talk to the Germans once they had been defeated. Nor would there be any sign language or touching, leave alone fucking and handing out candy. But as anyone who saw the first newsreels of American tanks rumbling into Germany knows, things turned out differently — grizzly-faced sergeants were seen flinging Hershey bars and cigarettes from tank turrets with abandon and GIs from Kansas sat on grassy river banks thigh to thigh with leggy *Fräulein* or held enemy urchins high in the air, grinning a strange conspiracy. Non-fraternization was dead in the water before the ink was dry on *The Soldier's Pocket Guide,* and for Germans and GIs alike, Eisenhower's proclamation was the funniest thing they'd heard since the war ended.

Walter and Alma were exceptions. They stood out in stark relief against a backdrop of flagrant anarchy. They obeyed the letter of the law, and non-fraternization brought them together by keeping them apart.

Alma had become a waitress at the Bürgerbräu Keller through no choice of her own. Her past position with the Ministry of Propaganda put clerical jobs out of reach, and she and her mother were living on stale bread and potato soup. They had no cameras, no Dresden china to trade. And no one touched Alma's body, Alma hardly touched it herself.

Each afternoon Alma wended her way to work through the rubble of the destroyed city, and at midnight she returned to the cellar again, slipping through the shadows, her heart pounding wildly and her imagination running rampant.

The clientele at the Bürgerbräu Keller was ninety-five percent American, bawdy and good-natured warriors, Zen clowns who still puzzled and awed the average German, and each night they filled the beer hall to capacity. Alma was not awed — she held them in low esteem. At first they tried coaxing her with words and touches, but she recoiled from both and they soon left her alone.

And then one night Walter came into the Bürgerbräu Keller and took a seat by himself at a small table against a far wall. He was making one of his rare attempts at diversity. He spent long hours working with orphans and displaced persons, but he knew next to nothing about what was actually going on in the streets, in the rubble and mayhem. Now he was seated in a public place with the idea in mind of drinking a liter of dark beer and eating a Schnitzel, and he was wondering just how to go about it, how to address the Fräulein when she approached his table, how to preface his order if indeed he should preface it at all, and should he look her in the eye and smile or would that constitute a violation?

Alma began studying him from halfway across the room, long before he saw her coming, and something about him came down softly over something inside her and all the configurations matched. She laid the menu in front of him without a greeting, and he studied it in silence. He quickly decided what he wanted, ordered it in very correct, inflectionless German, and then smiled over Alma's right shoulder. It was a daring thing to do, as daring as he was capable of and as daring as she could bear. She returned a smile into the corner of the room and turned on her heels.

Walter observed her departure in his peripheral vision and in spite of himself noted: big-boned, pasty skin, large bosom. It wasn't love at first sight, it was a fusion beyond their control and understanding.

* * *

By June of 1946 less than one percent of the troops that had been in Germany on VE Day were still there. The new troops were overweight, bored, and arrogant, and the Germans began to grow sour. Gone was the poignant immediacy of each and every moment, the acute awareness of transitory, arbitrary life that had been the premium by-product of the war years and had wafted over into the initial stages of defeat and reconstruction. The brief kinship between the American fighting man and the German people had come to an end, and normalization set in.

It wasn't long before the American families began arriving. The logistical genius that had won the war and achieved record-smashing disarmament was now applied to sending thousands upon thousands of American women and children to Germany. Commissaries and PXs were built, living quarters were arranged, and schools were opened. There were American hospitals and churches and movie houses. Compact wedges of

Americanese were driven into the cracks of German culture. Americans drove through Germany in big, fish-fin cars, peering out the windows and stopping now and then to purchase souvenirs.

Walter and Alma lived in a huge apartment complex that had survived the war and had been confiscated by the army to house American families. They lived in a two-bedroom apartment on the third floor, three blocks from the *Kaserne*. Walter came home each evening at five after processing orphans all day and kissed Alma on the cheek.

"Did you have a good day today, dear?" he'd ask in English.

"Yes, Walter, I haf had a gut day," Alma would reply.

"That's good," Walter would say, and then settle down on the couch with the *Stars and Stripes*.

They had a maid who arrived every morning in time to fix their breakfast. They ate bacon and eggs and drank Maxwell House coffee. Campbell's soup for lunch. The maid brought dark bread and dark beer in a net bag and ate in the maid's room off the kitchen.

Of course Alma spoke German with the maid. It would have been preposterous not to. That will be all now, Helga, she'd say. The bathroom looks very clean today, Helga. Delicious meal, Helga, but about the bedding. Perhaps we'd best not shake the sheets and blankets out the bedroom window anymore. It's not the custom, really, in America. Yes, of course you can have tomorrow off to visit your mother in Bad Tolz. *Schwerbeschädigt?* Crippled by the war — yes, I know. I, too, was in the war, Helga. And perhaps we can drop this *Sie* and get down to a more comfortable *Du*.

"Of course, *gnädige Frau, Du* is fine with me, if *Du* is what *Sie* want," said Helga.

They continued using *Sie* right up to the day Alma caught Helga leaving with a pound of butter in her net bag, and then and there they switched to *Du* and went at it out on the landing.

Up and down the four flights of stairs doors opened on a crack of indignation, and frightened American wives drank in the ugly, guttural sounds. Their own maids didn't seem to hear but bore down on their scrub brushes with renewed intensity.

After that, Alma did her own housework, which only served to set her off even more — she was the only German wife in the apartment complex.

* * *

Even as their mutual language switched from German to English after they were married, everything else turned American. The food they ate, the furniture in their apartment, and the very thoughts in their heads. Alma made this change voluntarily because she saw that order had been destroyed in her land. Order existed in America now, and that was where she wanted to go. She situated her mother with some relatives in the country and sent her money every month. She studied the ways of the American women and tried to imitate them. At first she played bridge on Thursday afternoons and visited orphanages with the other women, but she soon stopped doing these things. It was the same as it had been in her youth, she did not fit in, and something about walking through the orphanage wards handing gaudy toys to battle-scarred children made her restless.

When spring rolled around, Walter astounded Alma by suggesting they have a child.

"It would be nice," Walter said. He was sitting in his overstuffed chair and Alma was standing before him, her hands folded in front of her.

"But how?" she asked.

There'd been unprecedented confusion on their wedding night. There'd been pleading and crying and shame. There'd been no consummation, then or since, and Walter and Alma received their gratification by rubbing against each other in the dark while pretending the other was sleeping.

Walter reached over and with a frown began fidgeting with the dial of the radio on the end table next to his chair. "I was thinking we could adopt one," he said.

"Adopt one?"

"Yes."

"One of those you process?"

"An orphan, why not?" Walter said, looking up from the radio.

Alma did not answer.

"We'd be a family," Walter explained.

Alma stood rooted to the spot, staring down at him.

"Wouldn't you like that?" he asked.

"Yes, I suppose," she said.

"We could raise him like our own," said Walter.

"A *boy?*" she said.

"Of course," Walter said. "What else?"

* * *

"*Achtung!*" the orphanage director barked, and fifty children sprang to attention at the foot of their beds. Walter, Alma, and the director moved slowly down one side of the room and then up the other. It was a ward of five- to eight-year-olds.

They were mostly children who had been cloistered by nuns and monks during the war and then turned over to the state orphanage after occupation. They knew Americans only from the bombs they dropped or as a thin black line weaving across a distant field. Some still came curling out of sleep through the tornado-like funnel of nightmare screaming, "*Hilfe! Hilfe!*" or moaning, "*Mutti! Mutti!*" spreading alarm through the dark dormitory and igniting a brush fire of keening orphans. Halfway up the second row of bunks, Walter stopped and addressed one of the boys.

"*Wie geht's?*" he said. It was the first boy he'd come to who was not standing at attention. The boy stood with his weight thrown to his right leg and his hands dangling at his sides. He looked to be about five years old.

"He will not speak," the director said in German. "He is a good boy but in some ways difficult."

"*Stimmt das?*" Walter said to the boy, smiling. "Is that so?" He'd been dealing with orphans for over a year now. He knew how to talk to them.

The boy smiled. It was a frightening smile, his eyes intense and the muscles in his face quivering. "Sometimes, maybe," the boy said.

Alma tightened her grip on Walter's arm. The boy had answered in English.

* * *

Bodo was the name they'd given him, but at the Ludwig Strasse Clubhouse where he'd spent the year prior to going into the orphanage, they called him Bud. He was found by several older boys one morning in July of 1945, sleeping on the clubhouse doorstep, his eyes big and melancholy and his belly protruding. The boys who found him had arrived early to sharpen their ping-pong game. Playing ping-pong normally occupied them until the KP arrived from the Mess Hall with buckets of cold scrambled eggs and chrome trays filled with bacon and toast left over from the chow line. The KP would sit around in his whites smoking cigarettes and giving the boys pointers on their game, and later on other soldiers would show up.

When the war ended, there were more troops in Germany than there were tasks to occupy their time, and to keep the men from becoming restless, diversions were funneled across the ocean into Service Clubs and educational facilities. By August of 1945 there were 93,000 United States Armed Forces Institute students pondering everything from Hegel to Accounting 101. There were 21,000 basketballs being dribbled and much baseball being played. Over 100,000 ping-pong balls made the journey, 350,000 decks of cards, and fifteen million paperbacks. But still the men were restless. For years they'd been cultivating their ingenuity under the stress of war, and they resented the way the army was now trying to soften this ingenuity with ping-pong and correspondence courses. It was much more challenging to play cat and mouse with such absurdities as the non-fraternization policy. It was more lucrative to sell Mickey Mouse watches to the Russians and more spiritually rewarding to build clubhouses for the eagle-eyed children who were everywhere zipping through the rubble. The same GIs who were black-marketing coffee and cigarettes by night could be seen laboring by day to convert a bombed-out building into a clubhouse for homeless kids.

Sergeant Jansen heard the whistle from down the street. He got up from his cot where he'd been lying in fatigue pants and T-shirt, reading a paperback Ellery Queen, and went to the window. It was Joachim, ex-Hitler Youth leader, kingpin at the Ludwig Strasse Clubhouse that Jansen ran, and a good middleman for Jansen's black-marketing. Jansen slipped into a pair of shower clogs and went down into the street. He gave Joachim a cigarette and Joachim leaned against the wall of a building, inhaled deeply, and commenced studying the sky.

"Well?" said Jansen.

"Der iss dis kid at de club. Liddle kid. Haf starft. Dumped by someone, too schmall to get der by hisself. Vont to see?"

"Yeah, okay," Jansen said. "Let me go up and get some clothes on."

At the clubhouse, the boy lay on a Service Club divan. Some of the older boys had put a GI blanket over the vinyl cushions and placed a pillow under his head. They'd given him a pint of Mess Hall milk in a waxed container. He hadn't touched the milk and was scanning the faces around him. He did not speak.

"Oh boy," Jansen said. "We've got a real case here. This little guy is half starved."

"I told you dat," Joachim said. "But vot are you koing to *do* about it?"

"I think we'd better get him to a hospital," Jansen said.

When he said that, a silence settled over the boys.

"We can't keep him here, guys," Jansen said. "No way can we do that."

The silence held.

"This kid needs medical attention. All I need is for a kid to die on me and the whole clubhouse and everything goes up in smoke."

"Dey vill burn it?" one of the boys asked. A new concern filled the silence.

"Naw. That's an expression. Like — it's all over, closed down, *finito*. Authorities all over the place. Bad news."

"But he vill not die," Joachim said. "I haf seen much verse. Ve leaf him alone and ve feed him and pretty soon he becomes better."

Jansen looked at the faces that surrounded him.

"Ja, he ist right, you know," another boy said. All the boys began shaking their heads in agreement.

Jansen sighed. "Well, goddamn it, you little fuckers keep it quiet, you understand? I don't want no one, and I mean *no one* to know about this. Not the KPs or *anyone*. You got that? We'll keep him in the back room out of sight until he puts some meat on those bones."

"We got it," Joachim said.

Jansen squatted down next to the divan. "How you doin', Bud?" he said. The boy looked back at him with those unchanging, disarmingly calm eyes that Jansen had seen all too often during the war. He reached out and patted the boy's arm. The boy did not move, but his whole body tensed. Jansen withdrew his hand. "Yeah, okay," he said. "Things are gonna be alright, Bud. Old Jansen's gonna put some meat on your bones and turn you into a hotshot ping-pong player. You'll see."

He stood up, brushing his hands on his fatigue pants. "Okay you guys," he said. "Let's get with it."

One of the bigger boys lifted Bodo into his arms and carried him to the back room. "Let's go, Bud," the boy said in English. In the clubhouse, they all spoke English.

* * *

For the first three months at the clubhouse, Bodo did not speak. They had tried prying information from him, some clue to his past, but the more they questioned him the further he withdrew, and so they left him alone. They left him alone and soon he was on his feet again and wandering among them — eating, healthy, and silent.

Then one day, out of nowhere, Sergeant Jansen, who had avoided making even the subtle advances toward him that some of the older boys had made, swooped Bodo off his feet with no questions asked and sat him square on his shoulders. "Let's go, Bud," Jansen said, and Bodo found himself hanging on to fistfuls of Jansen's hair and ducking as they passed through the doorway and out into the sunny fall day, Jansen striding down the street holding Bodo by his legs, Bodo still not speaking but leaning down over the big man's head, his arms wrapped lightly around his neck.

They were in the jeep and careening through the streets, the shape of the new city pushing up around them, and then they were in the open country traveling north, and it was as if the war had never happened.

The moment had come as they both knew it would, and Jansen seized it with unerring, streetwise timing, a timing developed in a ghetto world where all mistakes have dire and impartial consequences. Jansen knew instinctively that a silence as formidable as Bodo's could not be breached with words, and so instead of speaking to Bodo, he listened to his silence. It was a grim story beyond memory that the silence told. Jansen opened up to the tangle of Bodo's emotions without demanding definition or explanation, and Bodo flowed into his life until their silence merged at a point where words were once again workable, and Jansen made his move.

They walked along the Isar in silence, and then Jansen stopped, took his fishing pole from its case, and sectioned it together. He had learned to fish from concrete embankments and off bridges that trembled and hummed under the steady flow of rumbling traffic, casting his line into a sluggish Cuyahoga that in less than a half century would bubble and steam and burst into spontaneous flame. That was home, that was what he'd fought for, and now he was at the enemy's river on a bank of rich black soil layered with fallen leaves, the water as silver as the sun and sweet enough to drink. The thought ran through his head like thoughts ran through Bodo's head, not thoughts, really, or if they were, so fleeting that they were converted into emotion before they could register in the brain, so that nameless anger is what Jansen felt as he cast deep into the river, and the whir of the line against the new and whispering silence of the country snapped Bodo into a state of alertness, and the plunk of the sinker jarred things loose, shards of already dissolving memory splashing down into the swift current — *moonlight, river, rifles, exhaustion, violation. . . .*

The one-word litany was so full of pleading that it caught the big man off guard. *"Nein, nein, nein,"* it went. *"Nein, nein, nein."*

Jansen knelt and lay his rod on the bank, his line going squiggly on the water, and he turned to the small boy beside him. Bodo has his hands over his ears, his eyes closed, and his body rocked gently from side to side with a delicate precision that alerted every instinct in Jansen, deeper instincts than had ever been called into play in him before, ever, even when they had him up against the battered and bashed body of the city bus in the wrecking yard at two in the morning with the knife to his throat.

Jansen closed his eyes and let his hands that had been journeying toward the boy fall like feathers in the still air to his side, and then he found that he too was swaying, swaying to the cadence of the whispered litany. They swayed together until the litany dwindled away, and then they were both silent and unmoving. When Jansen opened his eyes, he found the small boy staring at him, solemn and tearless, and they both knew that Bodo had suffered beyond Jansen's comprehension.

* * *

After that Bodo spoke, but not frequently, not unnecessarily, and usually only to Jansen. They preferred the silence where they understood each other without ambiguity, and they'd often go off together in the jeep, fishing the streams and rivers around Munich, hiking the lower elevations of the mountains, and eating *Gasthäuser* food.

There were two things Jansen never spoke of with Bodo: his own black market activities, and Bodo's past. The first because for the first time in his life he was beginning to have an image of himself that was in conflict with his activities, and the second because there was no quicker way to plunge Bodo back into darkness than to pry into his past. Other than what he cried out in his sleep, Bodo's past remained a mystery, and what he cried out in his sleep was stock-in-trade for war orphans.

As time went on, Jansen's main concern became keeping Bodo from the attention of the authorities. In the early days the boys lived at the clubhouse with impunity, but as things became more regulated, it became necessary for them to come and go like shadows. But whereas the older boys could ebb and flow without drawing attention to themselves, the younger boys could not, and soon Bodo was the only younger boy left. Jansen had fixed a special windowless room in the back that only he and Bodo had a key to, a room to which Bodo quietly retreated whenever a strange face showed up at the club. He was either in this room or with Jansen most of the time, and the months went by.

Life around them continued to normalize, and as it did, the irregularity of their relationship became more pronounced, until things were so normal that what had passed for irregular became illegal, and Jansen's friends began advising him to turn the boy over to the GYA for proper handling.

"Handling!" Jansen said. "Handling! What the fuck are you talking about? I ain't turning Bud over to no one for *handling*. Fuck you guys."

But as time went on it not only became more difficult to conceal Bodo in the clubhouse, it also became more difficult to steal time and requisition a jeep, and one day they were stopped by an MP patrol and nearly run in. It was that very night that Jansen made his decision — he would adopt Bodo.

But it was not that simple. It was less than not simple, it was absurd. An unmarried enlisted man with a criminal background wants to adopt a German orphan and take him back to the slums of Cleveland. Even Jansen's battle decorations didn't pack enough weight to pull that off, and when he mentioned the decorations to the review board, they rocked back in their chairs as if controlled by a single brain and an identical smile came to their faces. Jansen knew that smile and it told him he was back on the streets. He saluted, turned, and left the room. He went straight to the clubhouse. He was thinking on his feet now. He'd get Bodo and they'd *leave*. Go. Somewhere. Fuck this man's army.

But when he got to Ludwig Strasse, he could see from the corner that things weren't right. All the signals told him to fade, all but one, and that signal overrode everything and drove him straight through the open door like an arrow. A man in a trench coat looked up from some papers he was examining at Jansen's desk. "Sergeant Jansen?" he said. "Please have a seat."

＊ ＊ ＊

They'd come to take everyone away, a swarm of CID men and MPs going through the rooms, turning things inside out, smashing things, looking for contraband which they found everywhere. The boys heard them coming a block away and disappeared out the back door, but in their haste they forgot Bodo who was sleeping in his windowless room, and now he lay awake in the dark, listening, and in that total darkness the night merged with another night, and beside him in the bed was the warm body of a small girl exactly his age with his eyes and his hair and his blood in her veins. And he was a little man holding his twin sister and choking back his fear and already the silence in him had begun.

The directionless din beyond his door that had filled the entire house subsided and was replaced by something worse, something focused and cloying and evil. There were screams from his mother and feeble pleas from his grandmother and the harsh baritone of a language even more vulgar-sounding than his own, and then the moaning, the moaning and the shuffling sounds of many men deep in concentration over the body of one woman.

The door came crashing in and with it a swath of yellow light, and even before they hit the wall switch they began smashing things. Bodo lay still and the languages washed over each other and then the warm body beside him was gone and the room was full of light and two men were standing over him. He had been about to go out the window and into the blue light of a full-moon night, he *had* gone out the window, after they were through with him, through with his sister, his eyes not understanding, the walloping impact of the violation slamming at the very root of his dignity, and he sprang back in a fury and lit into them and they struck him down and he was up again, their harsh language punching its imprint into his mind, the smell of them, the smell of war, their crazed eyes, slashing and punching at them and for a moment overwhelming them with surprise, driving the scissors through the filthy wool into the man's thigh, and that's when they tied his hands to the bed post and took off their razor-strap belts.

They cut him loose and left him as limp as dead fowl on the floor, his back a bloody battlefield of crisscross lacerations, and then they returned to the kitchen and did the thing again to his mother and his grandmother, too. They brought up the cellar wine by the cask and poured it down their throats and the fronts of their big coats and their language grew thick and slow and they turned their wrath on each other, pummeling themselves around the kitchen, throwing wide punches that when they connected sprayed blood over the kitchen walls.

It was a force beyond him that drove him out the second-story window and down into the last of the winter's sloping snow, tumbling and rolling and then bounding barefoot in his flannel pajama bottom over the snow and the first patches of spring earth, the blood caking dry on his back in the cold night, leaving the farm house behind, light blazing from each and every window as he retreated deeper into the silence of the night.

"A little kid," one of the two men standing at the foot of Bodo's bed said.

"These goddamn scum bags will use anyone to peddle their shit," the other man said, and then they continued about their business.

When they left, they took Bodo with them. It took two of them to pry his grip loose from the bar at the head of his army cot, but once they'd succeeded, he allowed himself to be carried away without further resistance, rigid as a little corpse.

*   *   *

"How long were you at the orphanage?" Alma said to Bodo in German that first day, leaning across Walter in the back of the staff car as they drove away.

"What?" said Bodo.

"The orphanage — how long were you there?"

"I live there," Bodo said.

"Yes, I know, but when did you *arrive?*"

"Arrive?" said Bodo.

Walter gave Alma a look. The director had said it was best not to force their way into the boy's past. The director said it was a small miracle that he was speaking at all, that before he spoke to Walter that day, he hadn't spoken to anyone except one of the nurses, the one who gave him his name, Fräulein Hildegard. The director said that the boy had been hardened by a year in a black-market ring working out of a boy's club run by Americans. He had developed an attachment to an American soldier with a criminal record, but the man had been taken into custody and sent back to the states to face court-martial. It would take a lot of love and understanding to bring Bodo back to normal.

* * *

The director of the orphanage had taken a special interest in Bodo and decided to name him Hans. For two weeks the director tried to persuade Hans to talk, but not only would he not talk, he also would not eat. The director's way of handling the problem was to lock the boy in his room. Sooner or later he would crave companionship, and then he would see that to get companionship, it would be necessary to eat.

Bodo curled up on his bed and sank back into his mind. His mind was a constantly turning kaleidoscope of nameless situations. Things had no name and faces had no name and already Sergeant Jansen was being absorbed into this fabric. Bodo fought against it. His fight took all his will power and left little time for speech and food.

Perhaps Bodo would have died in that room if it hadn't been for Nurse Hildegard. She took it on herself to look through Bodo's records and found them to consist largely of the testimony of one man, a Sergeant Jansen of the American Army. Nurse Hildegard saw that Bodo's reality existed in the eyes of a single beholder, and without Jansen, Bodo vanished. She read that Jansen had called the boy Bud, not Hans, and she sensed that this was the key with which to unlock Bodo's silence. But Nurse Hildegard was a peasant girl with a peasant's common sense and intuition. She knew that Bud was not a German name, and she knew what a devastating sea of red tape would rise up in front of her if she attempted to establish Bud as the child's name. She lay awake at night pondering the problem, and then it came to her. She went down to the *Standesamt* on her lunch break and thumbed through their register of bona fide Christian Germanic names. The closest thing she could find was Bodo.

That afternoon Nurse Hildegard went to Bodo's room and sat beside his bed. She took his hand in hers and did not let go when he tensed. Instead she squeezed the hand, which caused Bodo to close his eyes and turn his head to the wall. She squeezed his hand again, and Bodo's head began turning rhythmically on his pillow. Nurse Hildegard sensed the rhythm, and closing her own eyes, began swaying on her chair.

"*Was ist, Bodo?*" she asked in a singsong whisper. "*Was ist, Junge? Ach, Du armer, Du kleiner, Du Liebling Du. . . . was fehlt Dir? Was fehlt Dir eigentlich?*" she crooned, coming through his defenses, her instincts bringing her unerringly to the small speck of childhood left in him, bringing tears to his eyes and reducing him to bewilderment. And then, without hesitation or anxiety, with total naturalness, she pulled his frail body gently up to her, placing one hand behind his head and the other at the small of his back, cradling his head against her generous bosom, stroking his damp, matted hair as he tumbled pell-mell into the warmth of her and the great sobs came bucking out of him, repeating over and over, "*Armer Bodo. . . . armer Bodo. . . . armer Bodo,*" until the name stuck.

After that Bodo began to slip into the routine of the orphanage under Nurse Hildegard's protection. His determination to keep Sergeant Jansen alive in his mind began to ebb until it became a surface, prayer-like exercise, and soon even this gave way to the slow-turning kaleidoscope of his mind. Jansen was metamorphosed into yet another black orchid growing in the dark soil of trauma, and Nurse Hildegard's seduction was complete.

But guilt was the digestive juice that dissolved Jansen's personality into Bodo's subconscious, and it was this guilt that prevented him from loving Nurse Hildegard. And because he needed her but could not love her, he came to resent her, and his guilt was compounded: he left with the American Captain and his German wife without saying goodbye.

✳ ✳ ✳

For Christmas of 1946, besides a Schwinn bike, a record player, a Monopoly game, and two toy pistols, Bodo found himself the recipient of a handmade doll. A little straw and cloth affair neatly sewed together and dressed in miniature *Lederhosen.* It was happening all over Germany. The *Jugendamt* was behind it. There were over 20,000 institutional orphans in the land, and they were put to work making presents for their parented American counterparts — in Darmstadt alone, 9,000 dolls were given away to the Americans, and the Americans responded with a deluge of chocolate and spark-shooting toy machine guns.

Alma dressed Bodo in jeans and a warm jacket, Ked sneakers, and earmuffs, and off he went hand-in-hand with Walter to the parade ground where the exchange was to take place.

There was a cutting wind that day on the parade ground, and the sky was indigo and cloudless. The children stood face-to-face on the brown grass in a double line that stretched across the width of the parade ground. Little puffballs of breath came out of their mouths and mingled in the cold air. A drum rolled and then snapped back into silence — the signal for the speeches to begin. For half an hour the children stood eyeball-to-eyeball while the speeches were made by drab men in grey suits and army colonels dressed in splendor. The speeches were in German and English and they all stressed brotherhood. The children stared at each other. Little Johns and Joans and little Hänsleins and Ermtrauts, all clutching in their mittened hands, a gift. Homemade dolls and factory-made toys. And chocolate. The German children were beginning to dislike chocolate. They had bad dreams about it. Already among the orphans, chocolate babies were appearing. This is what happens, the nurses and orderlies told them, when you take chocolate from the *Amies*. But here they were, at the command of those very same nurses and orderlies, and here were the *Amies* with their chocolate.

The last speech was winding to a close. A tall, athletic-looking colonel was addressing the children. He spoke first in English and then in a clumsy German that he had rehearsed for the occasion. He wanted to wrap up his speech by telling the little German boys and girls that he and all the Americans he represented were happy to share with them the gift of brotherhood. But when he got to the German word for gift, he couldn't think of it. So he simply used the English. Christ, they all spoke English anyway. For the colonel, getting up behind a podium and delivering a speech to a vanquished people in *their* language was demeaning. Unfortunately, the colonel had never studied his *Soldier's Pocket Guide to Germany*, or he would have been aware that the German word *Gift* had quite a different meaning than the English word gift.

"I and all the Americans I represent...." the colonel boomed into the mike, and the PA system began to sing a song of its own. Walter stood in a crowd of parents and orphanage attendants with an image of a VU meter on a radio announcer's console locked in his mind, the needle jerking over into the red.... he's bending the needle, Walter thought.

The colonel's arm was now sweeping the air in front of him in a 180-degree arc to indicate just how many Americans he represented. "I and *all* these Americans," he emphasized in his bare-bones German, "are happy — nay, *delighted* — to share with you, the precious poison of brotherhood...."

The Americans applauded thunderously. The Germans were stunned. Walter blinked and saw the needle on the VU meter disappear from view, and the children shrugged and exchanged their gifts.

* * *

Through the winter and into the spring of 1947, Bodo played American. He learned to ride his Schwinn and went to free Saturday matinees. On the lawns of the block-long apartment buildings in which the American families lived, he played cowboys and Indians. He was the only Indian on the block with a German accent. Inevitably he was captured and tied to the stake, or locked for hours in the basement stockade where victorious John Wayne types came to rough him up and issue verbal abuse. They called him Krauthead. Krauthead, Krauthead, wet the bed, cover it up with your mother's bedspread, they jeered. Bodo smiled, his eyes a steely green, his blond curls falling across his fine young brow. It was all a joke. They were only playing.

Alone in the basement stockade, he'd become acutely aware of the piles of stored belongings locked in the cyclone-wire stalls, the severity of the sunlight on the snow outside the high-up basement window, and how this severity diminished as the light slanted through the dirty glass panes and moved through a universe of dust, coming to rest in a shimmering yellow patch at his feet.

Then one day, with the coming of warm weather, the Indians were made to strip to the waist. Their torsos and faces were to be painted with watercolors to give them a more ferocious effect. When Bodo declined to remove his shirt, they jumped him and stripped it off. The children stared in silence at the map of welted scars on Bodo's back. It took them places. It spoke a language that deep inside they understood.

That night the children were especially good. Being tucked into their warm beds, they reached up and hugged their mothers to them. "My what a little lover we are tonight!" the mothers said, and kissed their children into sleep.

Bodo's mother never kissed him goodnight. Alma would say: "Haf hue varshed yourself hall over? Ja? Goodnight then." And Bodo would march off to bed in his freshly laundered pajamas.

By the time Walter was transferred to the states for discharge in June of 1947, Bodo had lost all trace of his German accent. He was an extremely well-behaved boy, never questioning what he was told to do. He found it easy to fit in with Alma and Walter, because like himself they generated a field of neutrality around them that insulated them from the rest of the world.

Bodo addressed Walter as sir. He had no name for Alma. He spoke to her in a yes/no fashion for the most part, and if he had more to say, he said it without salutation.

Alma watched his English improve, and as it did, she economized more on her own words that were indelibly stained with accent. Bodo's presence caused her to withdraw further into herself, and within a few months after he came into their lives, she stopped permitting Walter to rub up and down against her. She grew rigid when he tried, as rigid as Bodo when Walter tried to take him on his knee, and Walter stopped making demands on either of them. He spun off into his own private world, and even before they boarded the ship for New York, he had resigned himself to settling down forever as a radio engineer in Beaumont, Texas.

II: Texas

They arrived in Beaumont in time for the June rodeo. They arrived by plane late at night and took a taxi to the home of Walter's parents in Nederland, between Beaumont and Port Arthur. Stepping out into the thick Texas heat, Walter was riveted to the patterns of his past once again. He took a damp handkerchief from his hip pocket and mopped his brow; then, still clutching the handkerchief, he flagged the lead cab from a row of cabs along the curb. "Boy," he called, his voice sounding more Texas to his ears than ever, "load up these bags."

The Negro pushed off from the group leaning against the wall. Hands in pockets, he sauntered over to the luggage with a meandering grace that always struck Walter as insolent. He loaded the bags into the trunk of the cab, then shifted his weight to one leg, waiting for the tip.

Inside the cab, the driver threw the arm on the clock and the meter began ticking off dollars and cents. They traveled south toward Nederland.

Alma sat stiffly to Walter's right, and Bodo lay curled on the seat to his left, his head on Walter's lap, breathing deeply, exhausted from the heat and the travel. Walter absently stroked his head, smoothing his damp curls that lay matted against his brow. Only in a state of total exhaustion was Bodo so accessible.

Alma pressed deeper into the seat and stared out into the darkness as they left Beaumont behind. The windows of the cab were open and the hot air rushed in. They drove through fields of oil derricks, and the night was filled with their muffled booming, silhouetted steel arms bobbing between the moonlit sky and the black earth, rhythmic as feeding cranes.

"Vot ist dat noise?" Alma asked the driver.

"Derricks, ma'am," the driver said.

"Did you hear dat?" Alma said, turning to Walter.

Walter stared through the bluish moonlight at the vague outline of Alma's face.

* * *

The next morning Bodo was awakened by an elderly couple who dressed him in a cowboy outfit.

"You'll be a Texan 'for the day's out," the old man said. "Ma, give the boy a hand. Well I'll be a — will you just look at that back! Good Lord in heaven! Must be the Nazis done that. Them Nazis do that to you, boy?"

Bodo listened to the old man's monologue, his eyes wide, his head swaying in cautious response while all the while the old woman went about dressing him — the jeans first, then the embroidered shirt with the pearl buttons, next the heavy leather belt with the brass buckle, and finally the boots.

"Don't look a tad bit like no Kraut to me!" the old man said.

"*Jackson!*" the woman said, her voice veined with years of weariness.

"Well, he don't! Do ya boy?"

"No, sir," Bodo said, and they all went downstairs for breakfast.

On the landing, before descending the stairs, Bodo looked at himself in the full-length mirror.

"Like what you see?" his grandfather said, tilting the cowboy hat down over Bodo's eyes.

"Yes, sir," Bodo responded, slowly tilting the hat back again.

＊ ＊ ＊

They drove to the rodeo through a malaise of oil refineries, chemical plants, and factories. Names like Bethlehem, du Pont, and Allied Chemical flashed high above the enterprise, and the land stretched flat, endless, and humid around them. After months of being a playtime Indian and the recipient of cowboy animosity, Bodo's boots were now touching earth that real cowboys walked, and the dust from the arena where they rode bulls and lassoed cows was settling over him; the smell of Texas and the feel of Texas filled his senses and elevated him above the deprecations great and small that had been inflicted upon him. He was, for these brief moments, oblivious to the swarming, chaotic industry that surrounded him. He didn't know that there were only a handful of Indians remaining, and that the ones dancing in buckskin before him in the arena were bleary-eyed with whisky. He didn't know how lonely the cowboy's life had become. He was giddy with the transition, he was too many places at once, he was an Indian in a locked basement and a cowboy in the bleachers, a war urchin in the night, a — the kaleidoscope began to spin, spitting out flecks of color, subliminal flashes of Jansen and Nurse Hildegard and further back, nuclear family, flesh and blood. The hot Texas sun blazed down on him and the smell of gasoline filled his nose and the razored sensations slashed into the darkness of his mind, laying cold steel flat against the pink, dormant fiber of his forgotten past, so that something quivered and flashed hot before plunging to the safety of a still deeper darkness, rasping the air out of him, rolling his green eyes back and shutting down his mind as the first bronco exploded from the chute.

"Too much excitement," said the doctor at the first aid booth out behind the grandstand. "Put a wet towel on his head and keep him off his feet. Feed him chicken noodle soup."

* * *

Every day for lunch Bodo would come home from school and eat his chicken noodle soup. Eat your soup, Bodo, so your eyes don't roll back into the past and your breath doesn't come rasping out of you and your new cowboy hat doesn't get knocked down under the bleachers with the crushed beer cans and other debris. That hat didn't grow on a tree, you know. Eat up, eat up, put some flesh on those horrid bones. Let it stick to your ribs, make a man out of you.

No matter what, he always looked like a war orphan. Hard and sinewy. And those eyes. He made the other children peevish. Bodo would walk out of the red brick school building at three o'clock into the waiting circle of boys and take his place opposite his latest adversary. There was no doubt in anyone's mind that this is what had to be done, not even Bodo's.

The doctors said he was healthy as a horse and they didn't know why he kept rolling his eyes back and crashing to the ground. It was probably related to his hyperactivity. He was into everything. His first year in school he was a wise man in the Christmas pageant, leaning over the crib where the infant Jesus was supposed to be. But there was nothing in the crib but straw. He and the other wise men came from far away and shepherds came from nearby fields and together they stared solemnly down into the empty crib. Until finally one of the wise men looked up and announced loudly to the parents in the audience, invisible beyond the footlights, that a savior had been born. The lights dimmed and the curtain closed and the audience applauded loudly and brought the wise men and the shepherds and Mary and Joseph back to stage center for an encore. Bodo took his bows with his fellow actors, beaming into the glare of the footlights, and then he went crashing over into the pit. This time it cost him six stitches in his skull.

Other than trying out for every play the school produced, and usually getting a bit part, Bodo volunteered his services to committees. He decorated the gym more times than he could count. He collected large amounts of money for each and every charity drive that came along. He joined the Cub Scouts and then the Boy Scouts and when he got to high school he tried out for all the teams. He was a good boy and made average grades, but he was never more than a bench warmer. He was not popular with girls. He was at first abused and as time went on ignored by his peers. He persevered. He rode a wave of nervous energy that never seemed to wane. His favorite pastime and his one true love was hanging around the radio station where his father was an engineer.

* * *

Other fathers brought their children to the station, too — it was that kind of job. It wasn't like being an insurance salesman or a clerk in a store. Those parents seldom brought their children to their work, because they had nothing to show. These are my policies, Patricia, I sell them to people and if the people die or demolish their cars I give them money. Children weren't interested in that sort of thing. But if your father could lift you onto the heavy black leather seat of a fire engine and take you thundering through the neighborhood with bells

43

clanging and sirens wailing, or if he was a policeman and could show you his gun, cuffs and prisoners, then you were granted a special status among your peers. Having your father work as a radio engineer was still, however, a little too abstract to put you in the same league as the children of firemen and policemen. If Bodo's father had been a DJ, perhaps he would have been able to help eradicate whatever stigma was upon his son. If he had been the voice that prowled the teenage night orchestrating young love or had been the one who told cozy little children's stories to the young on Saturday afternoons. But Bodo's father filled none of these roles. When his father got near a mike it was to break it down into components of diaphragms and coils, and when he did speak into one, there was no magic. Testing, said Walter Steiner. One . . . two . . . three.

From the beginning Bodo was fascinated by the man behind the soundproof glass — he seemed to be in a constant state of agitation. His mouth went all the time and surprise, consternation, and sincerity registered in rapid succession on his face. He coaxed and cajoled a massive, invisible audience. Bodo stood with his hands in his pockets and watched through the thick glass as Jimmy the DJ gave the lead-in to a record he had cued up, then went into the control room when the record began to play and the control room mikes were dead.

"Hey, Bodo!" Jimmy said. "Beau Bodo him*self!*" he said, using the moniker he'd made up for Bodo. He spoke in a gravel voice, imitating Wolfman Jack, his idol. "You want to spin a disc or two? Come on over here and cue something."

Sometimes on Saturday mornings Jimmy the DJ would give Bodo a few minutes at the controls while he took a break. Bodo was at the end of his senior year in high school, and he already had his third class radio-telephone operator's permit. Jimmy the DJ stood up and stretched, wiping his damp forehead with a handkerchief. He tightened his tie and went out for coffee.

Bodo settled himself in front of the console between the two turntables, and while the Everly Brothers were rapping up "Bye Bye Love," he cued Jerry Lee Lewis' "Great Balls of Fire." He checked the controls and felt the excitement build as "Bye Bye Love" came to an end. He'd been sitting in like this for a year, but each time the excitement was the same, almost unbearable. He leaned into the mike and spoke very fast, like the DJs up north. He'd somehow never acquired a Texas accent.

His brief moments on the air throughout his senior year went relatively unnoticed, and what comments he did receive from his peers were usually condescending and mocking. No matter what he did, he was mocked. His peers seemed to be saying to him: We know what you're trying to do, you can't fool us. You won't get away without paying the price. What do you take us for?

As time went on it became clear to Bodo that he was guilty of some great wrongdoing. He didn't know what this crime was, however, and so he offered atonement in shotgun fashion, a wide array of services. And yet the more he did, the more he was ridiculed. In time he acquired the distinct feeling that others saw him better than he saw himself, and he began more and more to observe himself from their viewpoint. The matter was complicated by certain inconsistencies in different people's attitudes, certain contradictions. His teachers, for instance, were protective, as if he wasn't the social malignancy his peers took him to be but rather a simple mishap, something gimpy, pocked, and harmless. As for his parents, Alma treated him formally and kept a safe distance; his existence embodied too much of the catastrophic past for her to handle. Walter's attitude was the most benevolent. He would sometimes smile at Bodo while explaining some technical aspect of radio, only to have the smile fade into an introspective frown, his words trailing off in mid-sentence; at such times Walter's comprehension of what his life was all about dimmed almost to the point of extinction, and somehow Bodo found comfort in this. He spent long hours with his father, and sometimes when Walter had to go to Houston on radio business, he'd take Bodo along. They'd stay in a hotel and go to a movie and never fail to visit the 50,000 watt Houston station.

Bodo's grandparents seemed to side more with his peers. He had the feeling that they'd never forgiven him for fainting in his new cowboy outfit and losing his hat down under the bleachers. His grandfather simply didn't take him seriously, but his grandmother held a primitive suspicion in her eyes that frightened him and surfaced time and again in the entanglement of his nightmares.

But it was his peers' view of him that he finally came to share. Something about the harshness of it made it ring true, and his feverish activity approached panic as he raced to outdistance their animosity with good deeds and accomplishments.

"... Hey there, kiddies, feelin' fine in '59?" Bodo said into the mike. "That was the Everly Brothers with 'Bye Bye Love,' and I'm Beau Bodo sittin' in here for your good friend and mine, Jimmy the DJ . . . and now a little down-home music from a good ol' boy, Jerry Lee *Lewis!* . . . settin' his *balls* on fire!"

And he set the record spinning, the tension in him so electric that his muscles spasmed in his back and his face became one tense, brittle grin with green eyes flashing and burning. Perspiration beaded up on his forehead and under his arms and he looked through the thick soundproof glass and saw Jimmy the DJ coming out of the break room in long, loping strides with a half-full cup of coffee in his right hand, the coffee sloshing over the rim, Jimmy meeting Bodo's eyes through the glass, the look he gave a terrible mixture of Bodo's grandmother's suspicion and his peers' disdain, the look full of a sudden recognition of something he'd missed in all the years Bodo had been hanging around the station, the look telling Bodo that he would never again sit in for Jimmy the DJ now that he'd told everyone in the Golden Triangle of Beaumont, Port Arthur, and Orange that Jerry Lee Lewis had great balls and had set them on fire, and he didn't know why he'd said it, he didn't know what had forced the words out of his mouth.

* * *

Vaguely, while splicing some wire to customize the console for the new DJ from Houston, Walter wondered what would become of his son. You never know how they'll turn out, his own father had told him before losing his sensibilities. But a gas station attendant? The frown crossed Walter's face as he tried to put the pieces together. My son . . . a ga . . . ga . . . GAS! he was startled by his own voice, by the urgency and energy of it.

It passed as quickly as it came. A vivid, textured flash of memory. The hurried training. Men lying in a gully — CAD men, irritated, dirty, and middle-aged, clutching rifles and weighted down with gear they'd never use. And then the canister rolling down the side of the gully, a test being put upon them by some twisted, war-toughened NCO, the smoke hissing out of the canister, lazy and insolent, like the rattlesnakes that were everywhere.

Walter saw the canister and slipped into a dream. It was the same state he went into each time the barber put the finishing touches to his work, sliding the straight razor over the fuzz on the back of his neck. And then the acrid burning filled his eyes and he yelled GAS! just once before the gas squeezed his throat shut, throttling his second warning.

GAS! GAS! GAS! Men began yelling up and down the gully, some trying to free their masks from their gear, others scrambling from the gully, coughing and gagging, eyes watering, right into simulated enemy fire.

"What a bunch of goddamn fools!" the sergeant told them later, sitting in the shade of some cottonwoods. "Gerry would have mowed you all down like hay! What is it with you guys? You'd rather have your guts spilled out in the hot sand than have a little sting-sting in your blue eyes?"

The sergeant was hated by the men. He was from up north. The war was mixing things up terribly, bringing northerners and southerners together in incongruous situations, making white men rub shoulders with blacks. The war was demolishing the social fabric of the country. But it was a necessary war. Gerry had to be stopped. There would be time later to get things back in perspective.

Walter looked around him. It was late at night. The station was off the air. Just he and the janitor were in the building. He knew the control room was soundproof, but still he felt uneasy, as if he'd been overheard. Lately this thing had been happening to him more frequently. He wasn't sure when it began. He thought it had something to do with his mother's death, his father dissolving into senility. More his father than his mother. His mother died containing the suffering she'd endured all her life; his mother died with a certain grace that made Walter feel strangely secure. But his father was different. His father's senility terrified Walter. Made him realize that it took an emotion as strong as terror to register inside him. And then he never experienced the terror directly. It was transformed. There was a transformer inside Walter, and he visualized it to be much the same as the transformers he worked with every day. He saw this transformer breaking down terror that was quivering at thirty billion cycles per second into mild ripples of alarm. But the transformer was in need of repair, it was under terrible stress, and every now and then it would malfunction, allowing direct jolts of the original force to enter him, and then the memories would flash by in hot, split-second waves, obliterating his concentration, removing him totally from the

48

spot in time he had been occupying, causing him to call out a word or a phrase or a name, causing him to drop tools and once drive his car through a red light, colliding with a pizza delivery truck.

* * *

By the time Bodo graduated from high school, his grandmother had died and his grandfather had gone feeble and was living in a nursing home. Walter went to visit his father less and less and Alma never went. Alma was indifferent to Walter's parents. She was indifferent to all Americans and to America itself. America had destroyed her heritage, she'd finally come to believe, and now America could damn well take care of what was left of her. She didn't have time to visit an old man who dribbled saliva down his chin and pissed through a tube. The old man turned her stomach. The whole world turned her stomach. People no longer beat their carpets, scrubbed their sidewalks, or shook their feather beds from second-story windows. The world had gone to the dogs.

When Walter did show up on visiting days, he often brought Bodo with him. Bodo who now stood six-two in his stocking feet and was hard as nails. Bodo wearing faded jeans, workman's boots, and a green Chevron shirt. Bodo with grease ingrained in the pores of his fingers and down under his nails. Bodo the gas station attendant.

It was a small thing to do, make time for the old man. Bodo often came alone when Walter couldn't make it. The old man giggled when he saw him coming, slapped his thigh like he'd seen the old-timers do when *he* was a child, way back when, when the Texas Rangers were defending the border against Mexican incursions and not just dicking around keeping their image up. Before they *had* an image, the old man gave Bodo to understand in one of his more coherent moments.

49

The old man's coherent moments were mostly lodged in the past, like a bullet's trajectory brought to a halt against the innermost ring of a great oak. The closest he got to the present, and it was a great leap through time that brought him there, was the first day Bodo came into his life. His greeting, whenever he saw Bodo coming into the room, was always the same: "Well, if it ain't the German cowboy!"

"How are you, Grandfather?" Bodo would answer, but the old man wouldn't be listening, cackling and delighted with himself.

Bodo would put whatever it was he'd brought as a present on the night table beside the bed. He'd take the old man out on the grounds and walk him back and forth on the winding path, riotously lined with blooming forsythia. He'd sit him down gently on the grass under the magnolia tree and help him take his shoes off.

"Ah, that's good boy, that's so goddamn *good*. They don't let me out here alone, you know. Once they came and pulled me from a tree! Heh! Heh! I was way the hell and gone up in the tree and they had to go get one of them trucks with a carriage on a long arm. They sent a man up in the carriage to talk me down. Can you *imagine?* Me up in the tree in my pajamas talking to this man in a carriage! Well sir, I told him that if he thought I looked peculiar, he ought to get a good look at himself!"

The old man slipped away again, and an attendant came up to them shaking his head. "Sir, you know it's against hospital rules to leave the path."

"No," Bodo said. "I didn't know that."

"Well, it is. And look here, we'll have to get Mr. Steiner's shoes back on."

"Really?" Bodo said. "Why?"

The attendant frowned. "*Why?*"

"Yes. Why?"

"Well, sir, you'll have to take that up with the nurse at the front desk. We can't have patients sprawling all over the grass, that's all there is to it."

Bodo continued to smile, but the muscles in his back had begun to tighten and there was a quiver in his cheeks. The attendant shook his head in a final expression of disapproval and walked away briskly and with great purpose.

"Come on, old-timer," Bodo said. "We have to get these shoes on and start walking. We're in bad graces."

But his grandfather had drifted off into a deep reverie and Bodo received no cooperation as he put the old man's shoes back on and stood him on his feet.

＊ ＊ ＊

Bodo had been working at the gas station for five years. He wasn't much of a mechanic, but he proved to be a good manager. He went to night school and took accounting courses. He took over the books for the owner of the station, Jeremiah Rothstein, and Jeremiah opened another station on the other end of town. He paid Bodo a good salary.

Bodo continued living at home, and gradually he took over managing the household. Alma did not like it, but what could she do? She had never learned to handle things herself, and Walter was off in oblivion at the station, dropping his check absently on the kitchen counter each Friday after work for someone to take care of.

Alma took care of it. She stuck a good portion of it in a private account for all the rainy days to come, and the rest she begrudgingly gave Bodo, retiring to the privacy of her own sitting room to stare out the window as the white Texas days went marching by.

Bodo hadn't been back to the radio station since the day he botched up Jimmy the DJ's Saturday morning show, and then one day he got a call at work from his father.

"I lost my keys," Walter said. "I can't find them anywhere."

Bodo stood near the cash register with the phone cradled between his shoulder and his chin, wiping his hands on a coarse red rag. "I'm in the middle of a lube job," he said, "but soon as I'm done I'll have William watch the station and come on down."

Bodo pulled up in front of the radio station and turned off the motor. He lit a cigarette and took a deep drag. He sat in the car studying the station through the windshield. He'd been looking at life through windshields for five years now, and it hadn't been so bad. He'd never been more at peace with himself than in the years he'd been working for Jeremiah Rothstein. He was a man now. He drank beer and watched ball games on TV. He even had a girl. Joan from the diner.

Bodo went to the diner after work on Fridays to eat supper. All week he packed a brown sack lunch and ate supper at home, but Fridays after work he gave himself a treat. He'd go into the diner and order a big steak dinner. The same meal every Friday night, until one night the waitress suggested he try something else.

"Try something else for a change," she said after he'd studied the menu. "Why not pork chops and sauerkraut?"

Bodo smiled at her. "Okay," he said. "Pork chops and sauerkraut."

* * *

She rented a small cottage in a rundown part of town, and they'd usually wind up there after their dates. They'd sit on the screened-in porch on the wooden swing that was suspended from the ceiling. It took Bodo a long time before he could even hold her hand. And longer still before he finally kissed her. And oh so long, it seemed to Joan, before it broke loose inside and he pulled her to him, trembling like a small child.

After that, when they came back to her place, they went into the house and sat on the couch, their physical contact becoming more intimate. But none of it was as intimate, none of it gave her such a rush of fulfillment as that first night the tension broke in Bodo.

He finished his cigarette sitting in the car, hoping that his father would come out. When the cigarette was done, and his father still hadn't come out, he opened the car door and walked into the station.

He walked down the familiar narrow hallway past the control room and paused to look in at the new DJ from Houston. Bodo could tell by the way his mouth moved and by the way he was handling the discs and the console that he knew his stuff. Then his father came down the hallway and shook him gently by the arm.

"Bodo? Let's go home, son."

They drove home in silence, Bodo's mind alive with reawakened dreams.

* * *

It took Bodo nearly a quarter of a century to touch the body of a woman, and then he told her goodbye.

"Goodbye? What do you mean, *goodbye?* Why? Where are you going?"

"New Orleans."

He's going to New Orleans. He's going to the House of the Rising Sun. He's got a taste of it and now he's out to fuck the whole city of New Orleans. He's just like the rest of them.

"That's great," Joan said. "That's just great."

She stood behind the counter in her waitress uniform, her face drawn and tired after an eight-hour shift. She was holding a piece of blueberry pie on a plate. Bodo's coffee was already steaming before him. Joan slid the plate across the counter with a swift, frustrated motion, and the pie lurched to one side, nearly falling off onto the Formica. She ran through the swinging doors into the kitchen.

Bodo stared down into his coffee. Maybe it hadn't been a good time to tell her, but he was leaving on the six p.m. bus. Maybe he should have waited until he walked her home to tell her. Tell her on the wooden swing. On the couch. Or in the bed.

He got up without touching either his coffee or his pie and stepped outside. He stood blinking into the clear February sky. He wasn't thinking anything, just feeling the feelings caused by the mix of events in his life. Just when he seemed to be achieving stability and owning up to the cramped quarters of his own personality, just then a woman gets injected into his life. He comes down with yellow fever. He sees life through a yellow haze. Everything becomes warm and pliable. On top of the sense of worth and well-being that came from doing a simple job well, comes the warmth of feminine affection. All of it descended upon him in a matter of a few years after a lifetime of being emotionally battered.

Bodo looked around from where he stood on the steps of the diner, and nothing was real. Sleeping chambers of his brain were being roused into action. Dusty shades were snapping open and spinning on their rollers. The battle was resuming, and there were new alliances and fresh troops. Somehow, to compensate for social and emotional deprivations, Bodo's mind had bedded down with the mystery of his spirit and brought to life new creations that had grown to maturity over the years; then they had been lulled to sleep by a gas pumping job and a kiss from Joan. But now they'd been jolted awake again by a glimpse of the flashing hands and fast-moving mouth of the red-hot DJ from Houston. They stood in their long cotton nightgowns, these creations of Bodo's mind, barefoot on the hard wooden floor, rubbing their eyes with their knuckles. Soon they would rumble down the stairs, showered and dressed, to see what was for breakfast. They'd slow down as they entered the kitchen, hesitate before taking their places at the table, unsure about the new guests who had arrived while they'd been sleeping and wondering if there would be enough to eat.

III: New Orleans

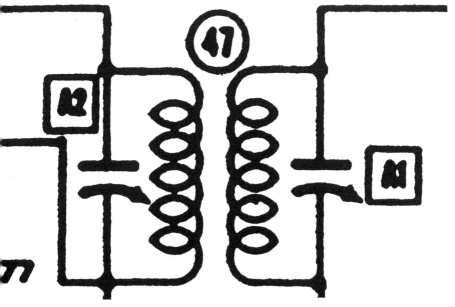

Bodo arrived in New Orleans early on Ash Wednesday morning in 1965. He checked his suitcase at the station and wandered into the French Quarter, walking close to the buildings when the street sweepers passed, squat, beetle-like machines with circular, coarse-bristled brushes scouring the gutters and spinning tons of crushed beer cans, shredded paper, and costume fragments up into their bowels. He walked down Bourbon Street past the closed strip joints and small bars and then turned toward the levee. He went along the levee, taking in the smell of ocean and creosote, and then stood with his hands deep in his pockets and stared across the blackness of the Mississippi.

He'd been to New Orleans three times before — as a small child with Alma and Walter, with Walter for a convention of radio engineers, and on his senior trip. Looking back on it, the trip with Alma and Walter made no sense. They never took trips together. They never did anything together except eat, and after awhile they even began doing that separately. If Bodo needed love — no one ever thought about love. Love had been put on ice in Bodo's life, love and self-gratification, and the beginning of puberty was a time of bewilderment for him. His first ejaculation was into the toilet bowl, he thought he was experiencing a variation of the burning business, having to piss but nothing coming out, only the burning. A pleasant, deep-rooted variation, an unreachable itch that his hand began working a rhythm on that gradually compressed the vagueness of the sensation into a single, intense point that exploded and permeated his entire body, caused his jaw to go slack and his eyes to close and his breathing to become labored. And then he opened his eyes and didn't know what it was. It was greyish and stringy in the water and several globs on the toilet seat reminded him of jellyfish.

He repeated the ritual several nights running, thinking that somehow he was churning his piss into a viscous fluid, and then he stopped wondering about it and performed the act in bed with the image of an older girl from school in his mind, a girl with big breasts and a long, smooth neck. He'd let his attention wander over the image of her but always just as he was about to come he'd rivet it on her neck, the way she used it by turning her head or tossing her long blonde hair from her eyes . . .

Bodo was fourteen when he made the trip to New Orleans with his father, the last in a series of convention trips they took together. Bodo knew the trips were something special, something formal and ritualistic, he knew it in his gut without having words for it, and he waited for Walter to impart some understanding to him like a fledgling waits for flight on the rim of its nest. But Walter was incapable of carrying his nebulous paternal instincts any further, and both he and Bodo were left with a sense of having attempted something and failed.

New Orleans had made very little impression on Bodo on his first two visits, but on his senior trip he went off on his own and spent hours roaming the French Quarter, gravitating to Decatur Street, the market, and the levee where he now stood. The magic of the Quarter got a hold on him then, and it was puberty all over again, a spiritual puberty, the same diffuse longing. The river was central to what was happening to him, the river was the spine of the city, heavy with secrets that were absorbed into the marshes and deltas to the south, sucked up into the smell of ocean and the electric sense of exotic places that came up-river from the Gulf with the steamers flying foreign flags.

There were no women in Bodo's life back then, on his senior trip; after the initial impact of puberty there hadn't been any sex at all, not until Joan. And with Joan sex was a by-product of something more complicated. Bodo didn't have the words for what she awoke in him or what the DJ from Houston and his customized console had rekindled or what it was that standing on the levee at sunrise made happen deep inside. His father taking him to conventions — it all tied together, it all reached back into him toward some central place from which he had somehow come unhinged.

The darkness slowly receded, and the shoreline on the far side of the river began to take shape. A fish jumped close to shore and the river was quiet again, moving relentlessly out to sea. Bodo retraced his steps to Decatur Street and went into La Casa's.

There were five people at the bar in La Casa's. They looked Bodo over when he entered and then went back to their conversation. There was a big pot of coffee on a hot plate, and Bodo ordered a cup. He sipped the coffee, picking up bits of conversation from down the bar, and then a young woman got up and went to the jukebox. She dropped in a coin and made some selections, and Lou Rawls began filling the morning. The girl remained at the jukebox scanning other selections, snapping her fingers, and moving to the music.

One of the men at the bar, short and slope-shouldered and in his mid-twenties, turned on his bar stool and watched. "Dardanelle," he finally said in a quiet, southern voice.

"Yaas?" the girl sang out, not turning from the jukebox.

"Why don't you come over here and sit back down?"

"Ohhh, *Terrance*, let me play *one more quarter!*" she said, turning from the jukebox and doing a little shuffle, her pigtails wagging. "Come on, Terrance," she said, "let's *boogie!*"

She sang at the Stagecoach Lounge every evening, and Terrance, her husband, backed her on guitar. He sat watching her now as she danced across the battered, dirty floor of La Casa's.

"You're gonna have sore feet when you wake up," Terrance said.

"Sore feet! Sore feet!" Dardanelle mimicked, making good-natured grimaces at Terrance, all the while jumping bowlegged from foot to foot in a parody of clumsiness.

Terrance smiled and said nothing more, and slowly the enthusiasm began to drain from her and she waltzed over and took a stool beside Bodo.

"Well *hi* there!" she said. "Where'd *you* come from? You work Mardi Gras?"

"No," Bodo said. "I just got off the bus."

"How about *that!*" Dardanelle said, turning to her husband and her friends. "He just got off the *bus!* Can you beat *that?* He must be the only person in the world who ever arrived in New Orleans on Ash Wednesday *morning!* Woo-*eee!*" And then, turning back to Bodo, "Where you from?"

"Beaumont," Bodo said.

"A Texas boy! Well al*right!* You hear, Terrance?"

"I heard," Terrance said.

"Lookee here! This boy drinks coffee just like me! Now here's a *smart* boy! Don't need to pump himself full of booze like *some* people I know."

Terrance twirled the ice in what had been a bourbon and water, and the others began talking among themselves again. Dardanelle turned her attention back to Bodo, resting a hand on his arm. "My Lord," she said, "I'll bet you ain't got a place to stay!"

"I'll get a room," Bodo said. "No problem."

"Well my lands, Terrance, did you *hear* the man?"

"I heard," Terrance said, looking down into his glass.

"Don't you think we could let him stay at our place?" Dardanelle said. She slipped from her stool next to Bodo and moved in close to Terrance, biting the lobe of his ear and running her hand through his thick black hair, her eyes big with innocence, her lips pouting little kisses. "Oh, don't be a grumbly ol' bear, Terrance Williams," she said. "This boy's okay. Don't you think I can tell an okay boy when I see one?"

Terrance looked down the bar, and when he found Bodo staring at him, he deflected his glance past the rows of bottles and out onto the street that was now golden with early sunlight. When he looked back again, Bodo had returned his attention to his cup of coffee.

Terrance leaned down the bar, peering over his thick glasses. "Name's Williams," he said. "Terrance Williams."

Bodo got up from his stool, hand extended, and walked down the bar. "Bodo Steiner," he said. "Happy to meet you."

* * *

Bodo stayed with Terrance and Dardanelle for almost a month until he landed a job as a singing waiter in a new establishment called Marie Laveau's Oven. Marie Laveau had been a voodoo queen. She had a formal unmarked tomb in the main Saint Louis Cemetery and an unofficial *oven* in the back-up cemetery in front of which Creoles and superstitious blacks came to paint red Xs on the pavement and say a prayer, hoping to make a wish come true. Graves in the New Orleans area were all above ground because of the high water table. The rich had large, elaborate tombs, and the poor were slid into honeycombed rows of vaults called ovens. The efficiency of the ovens was that as the corpses decomposed and crumbled into dust, new bodies could be inserted, pushing the remains of the previous body to the back. Marie Laveau had an oven all to herself, however, and no matter how many times the attendants came by with buckets of whitewash, the red Xs always reappeared.

"But I can't sing!" Bodo said, rocking from foot to foot, hands crammed into the pockets of his wrinkled corduroys. The rocking was something he'd started since arriving in New Orleans.

"Sure you can!" Dardanelle laughed, tilting her head and wrinkling her nose at him, and Bodo went down to audition.

Terrance and Dardanelle sat at a back table, and when Bodo had finished belting out Bill Bailey at the top of his voice, Dardanelle stood up and clapped her warm energy into the empty room. "Come in at eight," the proprietor said. "We'll give it a try."

Dardanelle went down to the Stagecoach Lounge and brought back a box of empty liquor bottles that she filled with water and placed on the kitchen counter, and all that afternoon she, Bodo, and Terrance sat around the apartment on Iberville mixing imaginary drinks. They were playing a game meant to teach Bodo about the world of hard liquor.

Dardanelle stationed Terrance at the counter in the kitchen, designating him bartender, and she draped a kitchen towel over Bodo's arm and put a funny hat on his head, declaring him the waiter. She hurried into the bedroom and put a pearl necklace around her neck and rings on her fingers. She put on a shimmering low-cut satin gown that she'd bought for a performance the previous New Year's Eve, and then she put a cigarette into an elegant ivory holder. She pretended to smoke while surveying herself critically in the bedroom mirror, and then she went into the living room and reclined on the sofa. "Waiter!" she called, and Bodo came rocking out of the kitchen.

Bodo stopped abruptly. His arms went to his sides, the tray going with the left hand and dangling there, the kitchen towel falling to the floor in a puddle of cloth.

Dardanelle was still caught in the role she was playing, her body poised seductively on the sofa, but slowly now her eyes grew large and her head began to shake as she lowered the cigarette holder. "Bodo, hon'," she whispered, "We just play actin'."

* * *

Bodo eventually became head waiter at The Oven. He opened and closed and had a hand in keeping the books. He was given an apartment over the bar with a balcony overlooking Bourbon Street, and sometimes in the evenings he'd sit on the balcony with his feet propped against the railing and watch the people go by in the street below. Every now and then someone would look up and meet his eyes, and the eyes of the people on the street were always restless and sullen. Bodo was both frightened and fascinated by those eyes. They told him something about where he'd been and something about where he wanted to go — routine had become supercharged with motivation, and Bodo was headed for the top, past the grip of gravity that never ceased tugging at him from the core of terror embedded deep in his past.

The regulars who worked and lived in the French Quarter regarded Bodo with fond curiosity. He was a bud of optimism in the desert of their wrecked dreams. He was dynamite on the floor of The Oven, and he didn't do drugs. His rapport with the band was solid. Night after night he traded jokes with the

Congo Square Voodoo Devils for tourist amusement, the sullen-eyed people with the harsh abrupt laughter, and twice a night he got up on stage and belted out Bill Bailey.

Waiters came and went at The Oven, but none of them measured up to Bodo. It was all the owner could do to get them to clap their hands to the music. "Let's get those hands clapping," he'd mutter to a new waiter while filling his order at the bar, but it was hopeless. Only Bodo clapped with enthusiasm. He paced and clapped and never stopped smiling, all the while working a piece of Wrigley's gum into flavorless rubber in his mouth. There weren't many like him left. The youth of the country had gone fuzzy and they were all on drugs.

Bodo didn't care what the other waiters said or did. His sights were on the future, and he enrolled at LSU in order to add depth to his background for the day he'd become a DJ. Sometimes after work he'd invite the other waiters and their girls up to his apartment. They'd turn on the TV with the sound down and put some acid rock on the stereo and some acid in themselves and lay back smoking weed and tripping out. Bodo stayed straight and was the perfect host. There was always a place to crash and a refrigerator full of beer for them to suck on when they were coming down. Often Bodo sat up with them all night and then drove his MG to the university for classes. He didn't need much sleep, three or four hours usually did it. That was all he could handle before the dreams came. Once the dreams began, his eyes opened and he was delivered into a jarring, brittle consciousness. He stole sleep like a fox stealing chickens, swiftly and suddenly before the nightmare farmer came down the path with his shotgun of bad news cradled in the crook of his arm.

Bodo fattened his life with the good things. With his color TV, his stereo, and his MG. He dressed smartly. He was always immaculate and cheerful. He had acquired a certain charm, and tourist girls from The Oven went up to his apartment with a smile. Sometimes he brought a girl along with him when having an after-hours drink with Terrance and Dardanelle. Dardanelle always treated these girls like long-lost sisters, leaning in close to them in conversation, letting a hand rest gently on a forearm, inviting them to come along to the jukebox to help make a selection. And then Dardanelle got pregnant.

When Dardanelle got pregnant, both she and Terrance were out of a job. Terrance played an excellent guitar, he was an accomplished musician and arranged all Dardanelle's songs, but without her he couldn't find work. He worked for a time as a waiter with Bodo, but the owner let him go after a month.

"He's too slow," the owner said when Bodo tried arguing Terrance's case. And it was true. Without Dardanelle, Terrance came across like a filing clerk. Like a dealer of rare books.

For a week after he had been let go, Terrance continued to come into The Oven. He sat at a back table drinking rum and Coke. At first Bodo got the drinks for him half-price, but then the owner put his foot down, went over to Terrance's table, and told him he'd rather he not come in anymore. Terrance smiled and walked off down Bourbon Street.

Bodo stood in the doorway of The Oven and watched Terrance disappear. Beside him, the doorman barked in the customers, telling them that the hottest Dixieland music this side of the Mason-Dixon Line was being played up on stage at this very moment, cheap beer by the pitcher and all the free peanuts your heart desires, give the little lady a glimpse of authenticity, sir, whatcha say, whatcha say, whatcha say . . .

The doorman's voice droned on in the background and the kaleidoscope of the street turned before Bodo's eyes that if you looked into them, you could tell he was in a trance. Then Terrance was gone, absorbed into the crowd, and the band was playing Bill Bailey. Bodo pivoted back into the half-empty club and went bounding between the tables over the sawdust and crushed peanut shells, clapping his hands to the music. Surprised customers looked his way and began clapping on reflex, and then Bodo was on stage, mike in hand, his iron body, his blond hair, his manic green eyes. "Won't you come home Bill Bailey, ahhh, won't you come home, she cried the whole night loooong," Bodo sang, and Terrance dissolved in his mind.

* * *

Bodo thought he was in love with Dardanelle, but he couldn't be sure. There were no coherent memories of love in his life by which he could gauge his feelings. But Terrance knew. He saw that Bodo had fallen head-over-heels in love with Dardanelle and that if things had been different, Dardanelle would have fallen in love with Bodo, too. There was a lot Dardanelle had to reject because of Terrance, and he saw that, too. Terrance saw a lot, that was his problem, he saw too much. He poured another drink and knew where he'd failed. He'd failed to lay success at Dardanelle's feet. He'd failed to make her star shine. They'd graduated from a small-town Alabama high school together. She'd been the hottest little number on the cheerleading squad, and he'd played trumpet in the band. They were both virgins on their wedding night. They spent the first few years of their marriage trying to fit in, Terrance doing the books for a lumber mill and Dardanelle keeping house. They watched TV and went to the drive-in and in the summer cooked out and swam in the river, Terrance sipping his beer and turning into a consummate chef, Dardanelle singing, always singing, Terrance sometimes accompanying her on his guitar. Terrance was a consummate musician, he was a consummate sort of person, and he was prone to ruminate. One of the things he ruminated about was their future. He began lining up gigs at roadhouses and in no time flat they'd worked their way to New Orleans where they hoped to be discovered. But a year went by, then two, and Terrance switched from beer to bourbon. By the time Bodo walked into La Casa's on Ash Wednesday, their dream had quietly imploded.

❊ ❊ ❊

Bodo and Dardanelle sat at the counter in the Morning Call, dunking donuts in chicory coffee.

"I just don't know what to do," Dardanelle said. "I never seen him this way. He's stopped shaving and his hair's getting all scraggly. He eats all the time and he's gettin' terrible *fat*. It just ain't like him. He sits all day messin' with his guitar and drinkin' bourbon."

"There, there," Bodo said. He patted her arm awkwardly and began rocking on his stool.

"Lord, Bodo — I'm gonna have a *baby* in a month. What then?"

Bodo stared at her blankly, and Dardanelle looked away from him impatiently and shook her head as if trying to snap out of a dream. "Something's got to be done here," she said. "Terrance is going to have to swallow that pride of his and let us go on down to the welfare office. You can't feed a baby dreams."

That afternoon Bodo drove up to the teller's window in his MG and wrote a $2,000 money order against his account. He went back to his apartment and poured himself a glass of milk. He sat down at his desk and addressed an envelope to Terrance and Dardanelle. He placed the money order in the envelope and sealed it, affixing a stamp in the upper right-hand corner. He went out the door and down into the street.

It was a clear, clean spring day, and Bodo meandered on his way to the post office. Jackson Square was brimming over with people, and he entered the park on the cathedral side where a young black with chipped teeth sat cross-legged on the grass near the fountain, flailing a set of bongos. A cluster of hippies sat around him, some of them barefoot, their feet black with street dirt, their long hair hanging matted and dull down their backs. Bodo stopped at the edge of the group and began rocking from foot to foot.

"Spare change?" one of the hippies asked, getting nimbly to his feet and extending his hand.

Bodo pulled some change from his pocket and placed it in the hippie's hand. The boy smiled as if he and Bodo shared a deep intimacy and then bent down to show the coins to his girl who smiled the same way. Bodo smiled back and moved on through the Square.

The Quarter regulars were out in force, and Bodo waved as he passed Horatio, the aging homosexual actor who could recite entire Shakespearean plays from memory. Horatio was sitting with his shirt off, his thin arms stretched along the back of a bench, sunning his pale, sunken chest.

"Ah, Bodo!" he called. "Come sit with me awhile, take in the sun, the glorious sun!" Horatio sat up straight with an ease that belied his years, waving a slender, graceful hand against the blue sky.

"Not today," Bodo said. "Have to get to the post office."

"Ah, the relentless drive of commerce!" Horatio said, closing his eyes again and turning his ashen face to the sun.

Bodo passed Ruthie the Duck Lady sitting in her one and only dress on the grass under a myrtle tree, a beatific smile on her face, her frayed canvas shoes lined up neatly to her left and her yellow duckling at rest on her right, its webbed feet tucked in, its eyelids hovering at half-mast. Ruthie wandered the Quarter with her duck waddling at her heels, catching the tourists' attention and working them for free drinks and money.

Bodo continued across the Square, and on the Decatur Street side he saw Jingles leaning against the black iron fence with his hands thrust deep into his pants pockets. When Jingles wasn't in drag, he was a slender and sad young man who wandered the Quarter in baggy slacks and a dirty yellow windbreaker he'd had for years, since med school in Tennessee. He was observing the upheaval of spring from a place of such severe withdrawal that Bodo's skin went goose flesh and he averted his eyes as he passed through the gate and out of the park . . . there were people in the Quarter who could affect him this way, and it was a good part of the reason why he stayed.

He walked back down the sidewalk on the up-river side of the park where the artists were set up and then turned up Royal toward Canal. At the post office he dropped the letter into the In-Town slot and then took a direct route back to his apartment. It was already dusk, and soon he'd have to open the club doors. He'd neglected to do some reading he'd scheduled, but he'd take care of that in the sleepless hours after work. There was time for everything in the rapidly expanding universe of Bodo's mind.

* * *

Bodo drove out of New Orleans heading west. All along the highway he saw hippie hitchhikers, sometimes as many as ten of them in a cluster, waving their arms at him in slow motion, their eyes full of disbelief as he bore down on them without slowing and they realized he wasn't going to stop. How could he stop? Where would he put them all? Someone should hire a fleet of Greyhounds to get them where they were going, and without fail it was California. They'd come to New Orleans from every nook and cranny in the country, and now they were striking out for Los Angeles and San Francisco.

They'd be lucky to get across Texas. In Texas the local police and the highway patrol snatched them off the roads, feeling up the girls and shearing the boys' hair, turning them back to New Orleans. Bodo had seen them leave and return. They knew Texas was out there, but they didn't seem to grasp its significance. And so they stuck out their thumbs to come-what-may. Some of them would even take along a lid of grass or a vial of acid, and their lives would disappear into the Texas penal system. They had no sense of survival. Bodo was thinking these thoughts when he suddenly hit his brakes, pulled to the shoulder, and picked up a boy and girl on the far side of Lake Charles.

He was hardly back on the highway when his paranoia came true. The boy pulled out a joint and lit up, sucking his lungs full of smoke and then offering the joint to Bodo. Bodo declined.

Their packs were up front on the floor and on the seat next to Bodo, and the boy and girl were crammed into the small back seat, passing the joint back and forth. Bodo's grip tightened on the steering wheel, and he broke out in a sweat as he tried to maintain an even sixty miles an hour. His glance went continually to the rearview mirror, expecting to see the flashing lights of the highway patrol. Unusual December heat waves rippled across the road. Bodo wanted to open his window to let the smoke escape, but he was unable to do so, just as he was unable to tell them to put it out. Put that goddamn thing out, you crazy sonofabitch, don't you realize what you're *doing?* You think you're free, smoking grass in Texas? You're as free as a lemming, a sheep, a slaughterhouse cow. You want the cuffs, the damp walls, the doors that open at someone else's command? Sweet mother of God, these people are doomed. But Bodo said nothing and they smoked the joint down to a roach and then the boy snuffed it dead against the heel of his boot and put it into a lozenge tin. He leaned over the seat and placed the tin in a side compartment of his pack along with the rest of his stash, then settled back, the girl snuggling against him. They both sighed and smiled their pleasure into the paranoid eyes that drilled into them from the rearview mirror. "Relax, man," the boy said. "Everything's cool."

"I wouldn't pick up any more of them," Walter said after he'd listened to Bodo tell about the two hitchhikers smoking grass in the back of his car.

"I won't," Bodo said, and they lapsed into silence.

They were sitting at the kitchen table, and they had drunk two beers each. It was Christmas Eve.

"Another one?" Bodo said.

"Why not?" said Walter.

Bodo went to the refrigerator, and passing the kitchen door he caught a glimpse of Alma sitting on the living room sofa in front of the TV, the picture on the screen jerking from frame to frame while her head bobbed gently in sleep. Bodo returned to the table, putting a beer in front of Walter who suddenly turned sideways on his chair, bent over, and began coughing violently into a handkerchief. It was something new, the coughing, something that had developed since Bodo moved to New Orleans. The coughing and the loss of weight.

Walter took the handkerchief from his mouth and smiled apologetically. "Don't think I'm up for another one after all," he said.

"It's all right," Bodo said, and the silence settled in again.

"Will you forgive me if I go up to bed?" Walter finally said.

"Yes," Bodo said. "I mean — I don't mean that the way it —"

"I know," Walter said, and then they were silent again.

"Well!" Walter said, suddenly erupting with enthusiasm. "Tomorrow we can eat out, seeing as it's Christmas and all. There's a special dinner being served at that new steak house downtown. You know the one? But not steak — turkey."

73

"I know the one," Bodo said.

"I don't think Alma will go," Walter said, lowering his voice. "But you and I . . . "

"Yes," Bodo said.

"It's okay?" said Walter.

"Okay," said Bodo.

Walter got up, leaning heavily on the edge of the table, and shuffled out of the kitchen. He padded up the stairs to bed, leaving Alma on the couch.

Bodo went out on the dark front porch and stood rocking with his hands in his pockets. The suburban street was quiet. Blinking colored lights draped lawn trees and stretched along eaves and porches. One lawn had a nativity scene, and another an illuminated life-size plastic Santa. He left the porch and walked to his MG in the driveway. He got in and sat in the dark without starting the car. He wondered, as he did every time he came home, why he did it. He started the engine and backed out of the driveway, cutting on his lights and driving slowly down the block.

He drove down the strip the high school students used to cruise. They were still at it, even on Christmas Eve there were several cars parked at the A & W. He pulled in and ordered a chocolate shake and fries from the voice in the metal box. A girl with good legs brought his order to him. He tipped her and watched her walk back inside.

He had the impulse to go see Joan, but he knew that was over. It was over the moment he first told her he was going to New Orleans. He hadn't known it then, he thought the first time he returned to Beaumont that he could walk into the diner and order the usual, but when he saw the way she looked at him, he knew. It was the first time in his life he'd been on the receiving end of such a look.

He finished his shake and fries and put his tray on the outside shelf. He drove back to the house and entered quietly. The TV was off and Alma was no longer on the couch. Without putting on a light, he got his still unpacked suitcase from his old room. He stood in the hallway and listened. Alma and Walter slept in separate rooms, and he thought he could hear their individual breathing, hear the sheets rustling as they turned in their sleep. The sadness hit him then, bluntly, catching him off guard. He closed his eyes and shook his head slowly from side to side as if denying some accusation, then shifted the suitcase from one hand to the other and went out the front door.

Passing the Lake Charles exit, he saw two highway patrol cars pulled off the shoulder. They had a lone hippie up against one of the cars, his legs spread behind him. The contents of his pack lay scattered across the gravel, and Bodo's headlights cut across it as he passed. He kicked the MG up to eighty and relaxed back into the leather seat as the dark countryside went rushing by on either side.

* * *

"Hey there early risers! It's ten a.m. here at KPMP, and this is Beau Bodo, sliding into first against all the rules! Yeah! Listen up now while Amos van der Meulen of Dutch Motors tells you how to trade in that sorry heap of bolts you're driving on one of those spankin' new hot-pistoned Chevy *Sportsters!* Then I'll lay the *latest* — and I mean *latest* — Beatles sound on your funky Saturday morning ears!"

He turned off his mike while the canned commercial was playing and cued "Happiness Is a Warm Gun." Then he shuffled through some announcements and cut back into live air just as Amos van der Meulen sputtered his last words about his super-special-one-day-only sale.

"Can you dig it? With a set of wheels like that you're riding ten feet off the *ground!* And are you ready for this? Do you really know what happiness is, Charlie Brown? Happiness is . . . " and here he slides into a baritone, ". . . a *warm* ga-ga-gunnnnn!"

And the music is right there, Bodo rocking back in his chair, nearly tipping over, rocking forward again, back and forth like that, his face covered with sweat, his hands moving from turntable to turntable, juggling records and notices and making log notations, suddenly cutting his mike on in the middle of the record and overlaying something like: "Oh, *yes!* Get your hand off *mah* trigger!"

He'd been sitting on the balcony one Saturday, reading the morning edition of the paper and drinking a glass of orange juice, when he saw the ad: *Wanted. Disc Jockey. Send inquiries and resume to P.O. Box 412, Baton Rouge* . . . He lowered his head an inch or two closer to the paper to make sure he'd read it correctly. It was there alright. Someone was looking for a DJ. He took the red pen from his shirt pocket and carefully drew a thick line around the ad. Then he got up and took the paper to his desk. He sat at the desk and began typing. A week later he had the job.

He was good. For the first few Saturdays he had a crowd of tense station personnel congregated outside the glass, but he handled the equipment like a pro, and although some of the things he said were a little off-color, when the phones started ringing, it wasn't to complain.

But suddenly becoming Beau Bodo again, for the first time *really* becoming Beau Bodo, didn't sweep him off his feet. He expanded his wardrobe and bought a 500 cc Honda, but little else changed. He continued waiting tables at The Oven and he continued going to school. He never felt more sure of himself in his life.

* * *

Bodo's money hadn't helped Terrance and Dardanelle. Terrance drank most of it up, and when Dardanelle began labor, he couldn't be found. Bodo drove Dardanelle to the hospital, and when Terrance finally got there, she'd already given birth to a boy.

It had been a hard birth, and Dardanelle was still heavily sedated. "What's *eatin'* at you?" she said from the hospital bed, struggling for concentration and clarity. "For God's sake, let me *do* something," she said, and took Terrance's hand and held it to her cheek. She began to weep without sound.

"Hey, little girl," Terrance said. "What's this bundle you got here?" He gently removed his hand from hers and bent down to pick up his son. He smiled then, and for a desperate moment her instincts gave her a shred of hope. But then he was putting the baby back beside her, its hands groping wildly and its eyes screwed shut, and Terrance's face had gone stolid again.

"You take care of that little sidewinder, you hear?" he said.

"Terrance?"

"You just rest now," he said. "Me, I have to straighten up and get me some work. Looks to me like this boy's gonna eat us out of house and home."

"Terrance!"

"Everything's gonna be fine, angel," he said, leaning down and kissing her. And then he was gone.

Welfare took care of the initial costs, but in the months immediately after the baby's birth, Bodo supported both Dardanelle and her son. First he made her a loan of $500, and then he dropped in every few days with groceries, a little red wine, and presents for the baby.

Dardanelle had begun drinking red wine with her meals. She said she'd heard it builds up the blood. She drank wine and watched TV and after a few weeks of trying to breastfeed the baby, she put him on the bottle. Bodo bought her a stroller, and as soon as she was strong enough and the baby was old enough, she began taking walks through the Quarter and spending long hours on sunny days sitting in Jackson Square. Bodo sometimes went with her, the two of them walking along in silence behind the stroller, Dardanelle smiling at him now and then, a new reflective smile. Once — without warning — in the kitchen of her apartment, she put her arms loosely around his waist and rested her head against his chest. He put his arms around her in return, and they stayed like that for a long time without speaking, just swaying lightly, like something hanging from a tree limb in a slight breeze.

Then one day there was a blues group playing in the Square for guitar-case donations. There were two guitars and a harmonica and they were better than average. Dardanelle got up from her bench and pushed the stroller over to the back of the crowd, and Bodo followed. She listened for awhile and then she began snapping her fingers and moving to the music. She crinkled her nose and smiled her old smile at Bodo, her head tilted to one side. "Bodo," she said, "listen to those boys!"

"They're good!" he said, awkward as a small child.

"*Good!* I'll say! They're *very* good! You watch little Terrance here, okay? I'm gonna sidle on up there and see if I can sing along."

In a few minutes her voice was blending in with the music, and what had been very good became electric.

* * *

"*Alright,* little swamp skunks, this is Beau Bodo signing off here at KPMP, buzzin' straight back to Texas on a *thought* wave! Flyin' where the *planes* can't go! Be seein' y'all *next* week, and meanwhile . . . keep your hand off mah *trigger!*"

He spun what had become his theme song, "Happiness Is a Warm Gun," signaled the live air over to main control, and came up out of his chair, his whole body covered with sweat, its dark color seeping through his clothing. He wiped his face with a damp handkerchief and left the control booth, walked down the hallway toward the entrance door. His suitcase was already in the trunk, and he spun up a little gravel as he left the parking lot and headed west to Beaumont.

Bodo went home nearly every Saturday after his broadcast now. It seemed that everything had given out in his father at once. His face was sallow and his breath fetid and he had aged twenty years overnight. Bodo had nightmares where his father appeared out of thin air like an apparition and hovered silently before him; and then, gradually, areas of his flesh began to decay like paper burning under a magnifying glass, going brittle and turning the color of light toast before curling in on itself and leaving a gaping hole. His father stood dazed and unmoving while this happened, like a wildebeest with its legs wide in acceptance after a pack of dogs has run it down.

Bodo would arrive and spend an hour or so treating Walter's bedsores and bathing him, and then he'd help him down to the kitchen. The doctors said they didn't know what kept him alive and that he should be in the hospital, but Walter was taking his stand as best he could at the kitchen table, sucking at a beer and trying to piece it all together.

"We've always loved you like our own," he said to Bodo. It wasn't true, but Walter was reconstructing his life to ease the passage into death, and work-a-day truth had little to do with the process.

"I know," Bodo said.

Bodo tried to change the subject, tried to make Walter recall the trips they'd taken, walking the streets of Houston and New Orleans together in silence. Looking back on it, Bodo realized he'd loved Walter at those times, and the realization filled him with dismay.

But Walter began reminiscing about his CAD days instead. "This guy Lambert — he was my driver! Why, he'd drive me wherever I wanted to go! Anywhere, you name it! He drove me to the Bürgerbräu Keller every evening to see your . . . to see . . . he . . . " And Walter looked up and saw that there were tears in Bodo's eyes. "Ah," he said. "Ah, Bodo." He opened his arms to his son and Bodo went to him, Walter pressing Bodo's head to his frail chest, his hands amazingly strong, the untapped solace left in him astounding.

❈ ❈ ❈

As Walter drew closer to death, Bodo's restlessness intensified. He'd begin rocking the moment he stood still and in class he could not stop from drumming his fingers on the desk top. Motion became more and more important to him, and he began riding the Honda to Beaumont for the sense of freedom it gave him, drilling the power of the bike through the great open spaces of Texas. Motion became crucial and sleep next to impossible, and he began peppering his broadcasts with random facts, history, and news that he acquired through his restless wanderings and voracious and random reading.

"Know the definition of radio broadcasting? The transmission of sound from a *transmitter*, using a certain WAVE LENGTH, to *receivers* ATTUNED to the SAME wave length . . . hey now, can you dig *that?* Do you dig my *message?* Do you know what's what? Who's *Who?* Here's WHO!"

And he sent The Who out over the air waves, music no one in Louisiana was listening to before he came along. He was beginning to dictate taste, and the station directors looked on, spellbound.

Walter grew worse, and the moment of recognition between him and Bodo that day in the kitchen was not to be repeated. Walter slipped behind a veil where he attended to matters that did not concern Bodo, and Alma hovered in the background. Bodo could not imagine what went on between Walter and Alma when he was not there. He wondered what they spoke about, if anything, when Alma fed Walter and changed his soiled linen. Alma made no effort to persuade Walter to go into the hospital. She made no effort to persuade him to do anything. She remained austere and aloof. She was filled with senseless scorn that she could no longer control.

Gradually, over the months in which his father was dying, Bodo came to see Alma for what she was. Alma saw him make his discoveries, and age came down upon her. It was the way she had always known it would happen, from the first day riding home from the orphanage in the car. Bodo was looking at her and seeing the miserable waste of her life.

※ ※ ※

When the group that Dardanelle was playing with had an engagement in the Quarter, Bodo took a weekend off from Beaumont and went to hear them. They dressed in matching outfits and had a van to transport their equipment. They'd added a drummer and a piano player, but the action centered around Dardanelle's singing and her energy. She came to sit with Bodo during their first break, flushed, smoking a cigarette and drinking a gin and tonic.

"You like these sounds, Bodo Steiner?" she asked.

"Yes. They're good sounds."

"You ought to give us a plug over the air!" she said, wrinkling her nose at him. But it wasn't some spontaneous idea she'd had. She'd been thinking about it. She'd talked it over with the band while sitting around a table in an after-hours club, smoking a joint and assessing their situation. "I know this boy's got a radio program," she'd said. "He's a DJ."

"Yeah? Where?"

"Baton Rouge."

"Huh."

No one was impressed with Baton Rouge.

"Maybe he could plug us," she said.

"Sure, ask him when you see him. What's his name?"

"On the radio they call him Beau Bodo," Dardanelle said. "Sounds a little silly, I know."

"Yeah?" the lead guitar said. "I've heard that cat. Picked him up one Saturday driving through. He's class. Too much class for Baton Rouge. Listen, I'd like to meet him sometime."

And so she had called Bodo and told him where they'd be playing, and now here she was, asking for the plug, drinking and smoking and lying white lies, and he turned all the things he'd hoped to say to her back inside.

"Sure," Bodo said. "I'll see what I can do." And then: "You heard from Terrance?"

"No, I ain't seen nor heard from that boy," she said.

"How's the baby?"

She lit a cigarette, crossed her legs, and blew out the smoke. "He's doing just fine," she said. "You should come see for yourself. You shouldn't be such a stranger these days, Bodo Steiner."

She snuffed the cigarette she'd just lit and got to her feet. "Here we go again," she said, indicating with a nod the rest of the group climbing back on stage. She went to join them, and Bodo left before they started the set.

* * *

Sometimes when he was in Beaumont for the weekend, Bodo would visit his grandfather at the nursing home. The old man was confined to his bed now, and they were feeding him mush. Bodo would smuggle things in — gumdrops, mostly, which the old man craved, and miniature flasks of whisky like they serve on airlines. The old man would down a shot of whisky, pop a gumdrop into his mouth, and settle back into his pillows with a sigh.

"By God, Walter," he'd say. "Together we could turn this place inside out!"

He always called Bodo Walter now. He'd stopped calling him the German Cowboy. The German Cowboy had been a novelty in his life, and he had no time for novelties.

"Yes, Grandfather," Bodo said. "No, Grandfather." And the old man wandered on.

"Would you like to take a walk, Grandfather?" Bodo asked.

"Walk? They won't *let* me walk! They say walkin's bad for me! You ever heard such a crock of shit in your life? How can walkin' be bad? Hell yes I'd like to take a walk." And then, lifting his frail frame from the pillows and propping himself up with his elbows: "You think we can get away with it?"

Bodo helped the old man out of bed. The men in his family were turning to rag dolls, drying up and blowing away. There wasn't even a bathrobe to put over his shoulders, they'd taken his bathrobe and slippers, and so the old man shuffled barefoot down the ward in his wrinkled green pajamas, leaning heavily on Bodo's arm. The other old men propped themselves up as best they could and glared at Jackson Steiner's slow progress down the highly buffed floor.

They'd gone about twenty-five yards when the nurse came on the ward and caught them red-handed. She took a deep breath in the doorway, held it, and opened her mouth in a silent, elongated "O." Then she pursed her lips, let the air hiss out, and marched on in.

Two orderlies put Jackson in a wheelchair and wheeled him back to bed. All the old men in the ward were sitting up now, and the room was full of heavy breathing.

"Do you see what you've done?" the nurse admonished Bodo at the front desk. She'd whisked him off the ward before he could even say goodbye to his grandfather.

"Done?" Bodo said.

The nurse had a vision of multiple cardiac arrests, a score of old men clutching their throats and breathing their last. Investigations and a blemished record.

"Yes, *done!*" she said, raising her voice. "Mr. Steiner," she went on, her voice low and urgent now. "You have been trouble here before. One more such infraction and we will be forced to deny you visiting privileges. Do I make myself clear?"

* * *

"All stories must reflect respect for law and order, adult authority, good morals, clean living . . . hey, hey, *hey!* That's from NBC's code of ethics, circa 1939, and this from the chipmunk pouch of the *cosmos* . . . Mr. Frank Zappa, no less, and a little ditty called, 'The Return of the Son of Monster Magnet'!"

He pushed the volume up and his VU meter flirted with red as Zappa bashed, banged, and roared out over the Louisiana airwaves.

" . . . Advising the kiddies to tell mother to buy the product must be limited to twice a program, says NBC . . . " He lays this right over Zappa's cacophony, " . . . contests which encourage children to enter strange places and to converse with strange people in an effort to collect box tops *may* present a danger to the *child!* Well, *yaaas!*"

Out there in the January bayous, Bodo's followers are getting restless, and when their parents yell at them they don't yell back as defensively, they mumble things instead and remain stubbornly faithful, waiting for Beau Bodo to come out the other side of the strange place he's been traveling through and show them he knew what he was doing all along . . .

* * *

Walter died a week before Christmas in 1968. Bodo had wanted to be at his side, he felt that there were answers Walter could still give him, but Alma didn't notify him until it was over. *Walter has died*, the telegram read. That was all.

In the months before his death there had been a transformation in Walter much more striking to Bodo than his physical emaciation — his countenance had become a mirror of his mind's final efforts to make sense of his life. But now, in death, his countenance had become inscrutable again, and the body in the casket bore no resemblance to the man Bodo had sat across the kitchen table from for the past half year.

He stayed in a motel room until the burial, which took place on a Monday afternoon. "Goodbye, Alma," he said after the funeral was over and the small gathering had dispersed.

"Goodbye, Bodo," Alma said, and a bitter wash of smile crossed her lips. It was the first time either of them had addressed the other by name since the day they met some twenty-two years in the past. The *Vergangenheit*. The long ago.

Bodo no longer spoke German, but the words *auf Wiedersehen* ran through his mind. *Auf Wiedersehen* and then *Grüss Dich. Grüss Dich, gnädige Frau*. Everyone knew what *auf Wiedersehen* meant, it was more American than German, but what did the other mean? It meant nothing to Bodo, it wasn't a string of words, it was *sound*, like radio static. *Grüss Dich, Gnädige Frau . . . Gift der Bruderschaft . . . Schokolade . . .*

A vivid, ungrounded memory surfaced in his mind, a wide expanse of dried brown grass, two thin pencil lines of children drawn across the field, facing each other, holding things in their mittened hands . . .

He spoke over the memory flash, like talking over Zappa on the radio. "You'll be okay then?" he said.

"Yes," Alma said. "And you?"

85

Bodo mirrored Alma's bitter smile, then turned and walked away, leaving her beside the mound of fresh dark earth smothered in flowers.

* * *

At first Bodo continued to go to Beaumont on weekends to visit his grandfather. He always stayed at a motel, but once he drove slowly by the house, the way a grown man deep into a career might do, returning to his childhood neighborhood, idling the car filled with screaming children past the old homestead, seeing it as in a dream, as a mirage on the desert of life, his wife sitting tight-lipped beside him, watching him drag the skeleton of his boyhood out into the open one more time, patient like a lizard in the sun, outlasting him.

Bodo drove by and looked at the dark windows and wondered if Alma was in there looking out. The house was a mystery. He could not imagine what was inside anymore. He could not imagine he had ever lived there.

At the hospital, his grandfather had sunk further back into himself and now spoke very little. Bodo had stopped bringing him whisky because the old man had lost interest, but he still took the gumdrops. Absently he put the gumdrop into his mouth and left it there. His glands, faithful storm troopers, responded. The saliva mixed with the juice of the gumdrop to become a syrupy solution that began running down the old man's stubbled chin. Bodo took out his handkerchief and wiped the juice away. The old man did not respond. He stared vacantly at the message being spelled out for him at the foot of his bed. It was Bodo's last visit.

* * *

Bodo returned to New Orleans and decided to grow a beard. He sat in class, his face covered with fuzz, and tapped his pencil nonstop until the lecturing professor turned abruptly and said, "If you can't desist from constantly tapping your fingers and feet and pencil, Mr. Steiner, I suggest you leave the room."

Bodo grinned and something in his eyes made the professor look away while he gathered his books. He loped out of the room, the grin stuck on his face, and left the door open behind him.

He walked off campus into the Ponchartrain Amusement Park. The park was quiet, the gondolas of the various rides wrapped and tied in canvas, suspended in their wild, thrashing trajectories, waiting for spring. A few of the concessions were open, and the one where people throw rubber balls into a series of concentric circles was doing a brisk business. The circles were one inside the other and situated on a slanted board; they were formed by curving plywood walls about six inches high. Inside the bottom of each circular wall, where gravity pulled hardest, was a small hole. The balls that the contestants threw went into these holes, which were uniform in size. As the circles grew smaller toward the center, the holes took on more value. There was a long line of stools on which the contestants sat. There was a narrow alley with gutters on either side that led up to the circle. There were nets on either side of each group of circles to keep the contestants from landing their balls on someone else's board. It was a game played in silence. A man with a microphone and wearing a change apron began the game. Commence playing, he'd say softly into the microphone, and the contestants would drop a dime into the slot to activate the scoreboard and begin pitching the rubber balls. When a ball fell through a hole, the appropriate score would register on the scoreboard which was located against the wall above the circles. When the time had run out, a chime sounded, much like an elevator chime in a big department store, and the electronic scoreboards ceased registering score. The contestants sat quietly with their hands in their laps while the attendant with the change apron walked along a catwalk behind the circles and in front of the scoreboards, determining who the winners were and what their prizes were to be. After he was through and the prizes had been given out, he walked among the players and made change, giving them dimes to feed into the slots. Then he returned to the microphone and began another game.

Bodo watched. After awhile the attendant, while making change between games, asked him if he wanted to play.

"No thanks," Bodo said. "Just watching."

He watched awhile longer and then went back outside. He walked down to the lake. He took off his shoes and socks and rolled his pants above his knees. He waded along the shore and once he stopped to stare at his reflection in the water. He tapped the surface of the water with his fingertips and his eyes became imprisoned dead center in widening circles of concentric shock waves. *"Augen,"* Bodo said. *"Augen."* And he closed his eyes.

* * *

At work they stopped Bodo from singing on stage. He wasn't satisfied singing Bill Bailey as he'd done for years, he wanted to sing Beatles' songs. He got up on stage and began singing "Hey Jude." The band began playing Bill Bailey before they realized that Bodo was off somewhere else. They ground to a halt and sat there with their horns and banjos on their laps, staring at Bodo singing "Hey Jude." He took the mike off its stand and really got into it, his eyes closed tight and his face twisted with emotion. At first the audience laughed, thinking it was a spoof, but then the piano player — young and jazzy and stoned on bourbon and Panama Red — joined in, and the result was so stunningly sad that the audience fell silent.

When Bodo was done, the lead banjo player stepped right in. "Hey, a big hand for the Johnny Ray of New *Orleans!*" he said, and the audience, hesitant at first, began to applaud. The band struck up some Dixieland, and the owner stepped from behind the bar and signaled Bodo off stage.

* * *

" . . . and here's that old war horse himself, Mr. Chuck Berry, singing about *his* — dig it! — ding-a-ling . . . which is *also* a field generator used for pack radios, kiddies, electrodes to the temples, electrodes to the *ding-a-ling*, dig it et cetera, *yeah!*"

And instead of playing that sad Chuck Berry song, he geared straight into "Maybelline" and set them tapping their feet out in Radio Land.

" . . . well chop your hands off for this one, baby! Upside-down in a rain barrel! Here's Jefferson Airplane, in town tonight, by the way, in *New Orleans* tonight, that is, in *striking distance* from the hamlet of Baton *Rouge!* Hey, kiddies, drop your napalm at the door in the Crescent City and dig the squinty-eyed cyclops, *Two Heads* on every belt and a jar of pickled ears! Hear those babies go for $30 a hit over in the Nam! Yeah! Acid *rock!* Bring 'em back *alive!*"

And the Airplane was singing that one pill makes you larger, while the other makes you small, and Bodo was rocking in his chair, the sweat pouring from him as each day he circled further down the vortex of war and Walter dissolved into the kalei-doscope of the past.

* * *

The dead and the living mingle in New Orleans. All Saints Day is a city-wide holiday, and when the old musicians die, the marching bands come out of retirement, a frail assortment of grey-haired old blacks. They make the long march to the cemetery, playing sorrowful on their trombones, coronets, and tubas, careful not to stop on the way, because if you stop, death strikes again. Marching back they dig deep inside themselves and dredge up their youth, work up that tired vein and slip in the thin needle of rejoicing, play hot licks, their old bodies swaying with a gentle grace and dignity, the sweat pouring from them and their hearts roaring the blood through their bodies. And sometimes it happens that one of them topples into the dust, and then the music stops, the musicians standing around their fallen friend, their horns at their sides. Then the undertaker prepares the body, and they must do it all again, children and tourists lining the streets, sometimes the tourists not understanding and stepping out in front of them with snapping cameras, the proud drum major in his pinstripe trousers and top hat high-stepping it and looking straight ahead, marching through them as if they weren't there. And in the bayous, when someone dies, the front door to his home is lined in black crepe, the clocks are stopped at the moment of death, and mirrors are covered over. The family falls into mourning and waits for the deceased's spirit to depart. It takes awhile. It doesn't happen overnight.

Bodo wandered through the Metairie Cemetery with its gargoyled angels and demons and its stone visages of the deceased and wondered about the spiritual chaos that must reign in Vietnam, the terrain heavy with mutilated souls. Bodo knew things. He knew that blinding and castration were standard forms of punishment over there. He knew that prisoners sometimes had their hands tied behind them and then were put face down into eight inches of rice paddy water with a choke cord around their necks, the other end tied to their feet so that death came from either drowning, strangulation, or a combination of the two. He knew that the Mekong Delta was a rice bowl and that the Golden Triangle of Texas where he'd grown up had also been a rice bowl once, until they covered it with industry. He wondered if they would also be successful in turning the Mekong Delta into an industrial park, the great symbols of industry rising high into the Asian sky — du Pont, Bethlehem, Toyota, blue smoke and orange flame belching across the stricken land. They were going to raze the jungles and do it, there was no doubt about it. Troubled, Bodo left the cemetery and rode his Honda back into the Quarter.

He parked in the courtyard behind The Oven and went up the back stairs to his apartment. There was a telegram stuck under his door. He sat on the balcony and read it, using his index finger to rip the yellow envelope open. *Your grandfather has died*, Alma told the man at Western Union, and he relayed the message from Beaumont to New Orleans.

* * *

The next Saturday he let his theme song play all the way through and then he let a few seconds of dead air go by before saying, "Hey kiddies! How's *your* grand-pappy? Happiness, happiness, happiness . . . Did you know that Al Jolson *didn't* — I repeat, *didn't* — make the first talkie movie? No sir. The first talkie was put together by a madman named Lee de Forest, and it starred a black piano player named Eubie Blake. That's right, ladies and gentlemen, sad as it may sound. Speaking of sound, Mr. de Forest also did the first radio broadcast back in 1910. He broadcasted the voice of the Great Caruso from the stage of the Metropolitan Opera all the way to the lobby! With the doors open you could hear Enrico three blocks away, but with the aid of radio, you could barely pick him up in the lobby! Hey, what? Say what? It's the old John Henry story *all over again!* All the news that's fit to print! The rrrr EST of the story! Chin up, cheer up, hands up — happiness is a warm ga-ga-*gunnnnn!*"

And the record is spinning, Little Richard doing "Rip It Up," more and more he's playing '50s music and more and more his ratings are falling. After "Rip It Up" he goes right into "Lucille," and from there straight into "Long Tall Sally," the engineer at the glass giving hand signals, he's riding right over commercials, station identification, and now he's playing "The Great Pretender" and doesn't seem to be there, seems to be dreaming until (suddenly cutting into the music) — " . . . yes, yes, yes, YES! We are *all* great pretenders! These words now from none other than Colonel George Patton III: 'I *do* like to see the arms and legs *fly!*' Also, says George: 'Find the bastards and pile on!' Not to mention: 'The present ratio of ninety percent killing and ten percent pacification is *just about right!*' Not to mention . . . "

But he's off the air. They've cut him from main control, telling the listening audience that they're having technical difficulties, please stand by, and instead of Beau Bodo going out over the air, it's Mantovani and a thousand strings.

" . . . did you know that every Special Forces soldier in Nam has *three* bodyguards? Nungs they're called, and if you throw a grenade at a Special Forces soldier, a Nung will *fall* on it! Oh, *yes!*"

And then he realizes that his console has gone dead. He sits back in his chair, not rocking now. He takes a handkerchief from his hip pocket and wipes his face. He gets up and leaves the control room door open behind him, walks from the station. He starts the Honda and idles out into traffic.

* * *

Bodo comes down into the streets of the Quarter after sleeping late, having drunk too much the night before. He's missed class again. He's begun drinking to excess, and it has allowed him to sleep more than he's ever slept in his life. I'll drop out, he thinks. I don't need it. I'm Beau Bodo. My sound waves convert into electromagnetic waves and flash away at the speed of light . . .

He stops short as he approaches the MG. The night before he'd taken a girl from The Oven out to Lake Ponchartrain. They'd mostly talked. He'd talked, anyway. He had some ideas to express. He'd taken the girl back to her hotel about three in the morning and left the car on the street with the top down. Apparently. The top was down now. And the stuffing was sticking out of the seats and was all over the floor and on the sidewalk beside the car. Someone had climbed into the car with a knife and slashed the leather seats. Spanish moss, Bodo thinks. They stuff car seats with Spanish moss. Spanish moss is related to the pineapple and it feeds on air. A pineapple is a fragmentation bomb that covers over five football fields with shards of metal. He laughs and walks off toward the Morning Call for chicory coffee and a beignet.

Passing through Jackson Square, he finds Horatio, throwing Frisbee with Jingles. Jingles, the queen of queens. When Jingles gets dressed up, she's beautiful. She takes a lot of drunk sailors home and suffers a lot of abuse when they discover what she really is. Other men fall in love with her, send her gifts, protect her when she's in danger. Jingles throws a good Frisbee, and Horatio is bounding off across the grass like a gazelle after a high toss. Bodo intercepts the Frisbee, snatches it out of the air and snaps it back towards Jingles. Jingles leaps straight up and pulls the orange disc down from the blue sky.

"Nice throw!" Jingles calls.

"My, my!" Horatio says. "Look at Bodo! Such skill!"

Bodo is upside down and walking on his hands, while across the Square, fingering the Frisbee, Jingles smiles his sad smile.

"Where's ya shoes?" Ruthie the Duck Lady calls to Bodo from her bench. Something is wrong with Ruthie's feet, they're swollen and discolored, and she's very aware of shoes.

"Home!" Bodo says, springing to his feet. Bodo has left his apartment without shoes. He has on old jeans and a T-shirt. He throws Frisbee awhile with Horatio and Jingles, and then he walks down Royal toward Esplanade.

* * *

"Hey, boy!" What you doin' in here? Lord, Bodo, I ain't seen you in a coon's age! My *lands!* What's that you got all over your face?"

Bodo looks up from his drink and Dardanelle is leaning against him, resting an arm comfortably on his shoulder.

"You been drinking?" he asks.

She laughs. "Bet your booties, hon!" she says. "Y'all come on over here and join us."

She leads him across the crowded bar to a small table in a corner. She introduces him to a large black man in expensive clothes. "This here's Winthrop," she says. "He's gonna be my agent."

"Your agent?" Bodo says. He forgets to shake Winthrop's hand, and Winthrop withdraws it with the slow precision of a twenty-inch gun being wheeled back into its camouflage.

"Yes!" Dardanelle says.

"What do you need an agent for?"

"Oh, you're thinkin' of them boys I was singin' with. I wasn't goin' nowhere with them boys, Bodo. Winthrop here, he's got *connections,* and he's gonna *take* me places. Ain't that right, Winthrop?"

Winthrop smiles but does not say anything. Bodo stares at him, and Winthrop, his eyes hooded, stares calmly back. Bodo looks back to Dardanelle.

"What about the baby?"

"Lord, Bodo," she says, "you're just like someone's grandma. Terrance Junior is hardly a baby anymore. And besides, just don't you worry about me and mine, you hear?" She says it with a warning in her voice.

Bodo goes around with them from bar to bar and then they go to Winthrop's place uptown. For Bodo, crossing Canal Street with a purpose other than going to classes or getting out of town is like dropping off the edge of the earth.

There are other people already at the apartment, but Bodo doesn't know any of them, he doesn't know this world Dardanelle has brought him into at all. Dardanelle, on the other hand, seems to move among these people with ease, but then, Bodo thinks, she's always been able to do that no matter where she goes. She introduces him as Beau Bodo and everyone is polite and shakes his hand but no one knows who he is and they don't care. Beau Bodo sounds ridiculous to his ears when Dardanelle says it.

He sits quietly in a corner by the stereo drinking whisky. The music is black and foreign to him, and before long the room begins to rock gently, and he goes unsteadily to the kitchen and puts on water for coffee. While he's waiting for the water to boil, Dardanelle passes through on her way back from the bathroom.

"Hey," she says, coming over to him, "you makin' yourself right at home, ain't ya?" She moves in close to him.

"Where's Terrance?" Bodo asks, and Dardanelle's eyes close as if she'd received one of Alma's telegrams; she puts her arms loosely around Bodo's waist like she did one day a long time ago, and just then the water begins to boil. Without saying anything, and leaving the water whistling on the burner, she takes Bodo by the hand down the hallway and into a dark room. She moves close to him again, undoes his shirt, and places her face against his chest, running her hands under the shirt and over his bare back.

"Lordy, lordy," she moans. "What happened to your *back?*"

"What?" Bodo says. His head is still spinning from the whisky, and foreign sounds are running through his head in stringers.

"Your back," she says. "What happened?"

"My back?"

"Hey," she says, and she begins moving against him with a tenderness that has no place to go now that they've taken her baby from her and Terrance has entered another world, pulling a child's wagon through the streets of Mobile, selling firewood by the bundle to the poor.

Afterwards they go back into the living room. A joint is being passed around, and Winthrop hands it to Bodo as he enters the room. "Good shit," Winthrop says, still holding smoke in his lungs.

Bodo takes the joint and draws on it, coughs. People around the room look preoccupied with small things like tapping ash into an ashtray or buttoning a button, as if they hadn't noticed the cough.

"I never smoked before," Bodo explains, and he tries again.

The joint goes around once more and then another is lit and gradually Bodo manages to keep some smoke down. Then, suddenly (and yet slowly) a curtain seems to lift, and he finds he is seeing everyone in the room, seeing the room itself as if for the first time, as if he had just been jettisoned from a womb through a roaring red tunnel. Sounds are more precise, vision is lucid, things are sharply etched, and there is a total cognizance of *everything,* so that when he looks into Winthrop's eyes,

Winthrop is no longer an enigma to him but an open, under-standable book.

"Holy shit!" Bodo says, rocking now, the grin on his face, more intense than ever. "I've just come tumbling out of a *womb!*" And they all laugh but not for the reason Bodo thinks.

Across the room he sees Dardanelle, laughing like the rest, taking a white powder up her nostril from a pocket mirror, and a vision rolls through his mind more vivid than anything he's ever experienced before: a white cottontail rabbit bound-ing soundlessly through deep snow, the snow flying up in silent spurts, the entire vision without sound until the rabbit comes down on a steel-grey trap that stands out in harsh relief against the blinding white snow. There is a fringe of jagged mountains far off on the horizon and gnarled black trees twisting up into a cobalt-blue sky, and then the brutal sound of snapping bone shatters the silence and there is an explosion of scarlet. As if Bodo's eyes were the lens of a camera, blood begins running in rust-colored washes down his retina . . .

Bodo sits down heavily on a chair. He looks around him and realizes that no one has noticed anything and that the conversations in the room are continuing much the same as before. He realizes that hardly any time has gone by at all, and then he takes the joint that is being held out to him and fills his lungs with smoke again.

＊ ＊ ＊

Bodo washed out of school and was disenfranchised at the station, but he shaved the fuzz off his face and leveled out enough to hold his job at The Oven. He began singing Bill Bailey again and doing his routine, and the owner relaxed — what Bodo did off duty was his own business.

Off duty he'd begun hanging around with Bert, a new waiter who'd come down from San Francisco. The two of them would sit around Bodo's apartment drinking beer and smoking grass after the club closed, and Bodo's mind would run away with him. Every time he smoked grass it was like that. He pursued his thoughts staccato-fashion and Bert threw out obstacles, fencing Bodo in and eventually backing him into a deep trench of inadequacy. Bert was in his early thirties, and he'd been around. A hundred odd jobs and lots of institutions. He'd even attended a police academy. But no matter how he tried, he couldn't get with the Program. It was a wasteland of hypocrisy, and so he dropped out. He dropped out of the straight world and he dropped out of the counterculture and the only thing he fell back on from time to time was Zen. "Zen's got it," he told Bodo, "because it *hasn't* got it. Dig this: 'In the spring rain, a small child's ball is getting wet on the roof.' If you can *feel* that, if the essence of that gets under your skin, then you know everything there is to know. The rest is illusion, and there's nothing left but to sit back, light up a number, and let the days go by."

Bodo sat ramrod straight on his floor cushion across from Bert. Bert was introducing him to new ideas and concepts, forcing him to delve into a mountain of books in order to hold his own in their early-morning conversations. Time and again Bodo would oppose him, using information he'd acquired just that day, only to find himself subdued by the time the first hint of light was in the sky, sitting quietly and listening to Bert reel out still another spontaneous interpretation of life's true meaning. Bodo knew Bert would step back as soon as he'd finished, happy and surprised, saying, in effect: "Look at that! Isn't that something! My Lord, where did *that* come from?" And then he would be gone, taking the happiness with him, the happiness being rooted in the act of creation not in the creation itself which was left behind for Bodo to fret over and laboriously dismantle, piece by analytical piece.

When in a few months Bert disappeared as suddenly as he'd arrived, walking off the floor with his bank money on a slow Thursday night, Bodo experienced a bewildering vacuum inside that was eventually replaced with a turbulent relief the night he met Fran. Fran was on the run. She was running from a rich daddy, a nursing school, and Ted. Her daddy was rich and Ted's daddy was rich and richness bored her. She wanted thrills. She wanted this electric madman singing Bill Bailey up on stage. She wanted what lay behind those insane eyes.

She was dressed in some sort of powder-blue gossamer dress that floated and caressed her body. Her body was young and ripe and her skin was smooth and the color of honey. Her hair was blonde and full of summer heat. Later, in Bodo's apartment, standing beside the bed, she took off his arm garters and string tie and undid the buttons of his short-sleeved white shirt. Bodo's body was hard and also the color of honey and she held him lightly by the waist and tongued and sucked his nipples erect and no one had ever done anything like that to him, not ever, and something exploded inside.

He snapped the clasp at the back of her dress and it drifted from her like a cloud. She was naked. She was naked and sliding Bodo's shirt back over his shoulders and he was kissing her, nipping at her, sucking her nipples hard, and then he was on his knees and she had fistfuls of his hair, her face turned to the ceiling, her eyes closed, smiling . . .

* * *

At night after closing he'd go up to the apartment and she'd be lying on the bed in her negligee, reading a romance or some cheap mystery, and they'd make love and in the morning make love again and often after making love lie in each other's arms and talk about their lives.

"Tell me about some of your girlfriends," Fran would say. "You can't tell me you didn't have a *slew*, Bodo Steiner."

So he told her about Joan as best he could, but he could not make her come to life. He could not make any of it come to life, and the more she tried to get him to talk about his past, the more distant he grew, and she did not like the distance. She'd come for excitement and thrills, and so she stopped wondering about Bodo's past and listened to his stories about Bert. Bert was the tip of the iceberg, that's what she didn't understand, it all lay connected end-to-end under the surface and stretched back into the past, and it wasn't just Bert that Bodo was hanging onto, it was the invisible past connected to him. He was hanging on to Bert and he was hanging on to Fran because he was growing tired of having things dissolve and run through his fingers like water; a premonition of where it was all leading had begun to form in him, and he did not want to go to that place.

Often in the afternoons they'd leave the comfort of the air-conditioned apartment and walk through the Quarter, stopping to eat seafood or maybe sit in the Napoleon House and drink mint juleps. Sometimes they'd play chess, which neither of them did very well, and sometimes they'd go to the levee and Bodo would try to explain what it was like for him to be there at sunrise. Fran listened while scratching in the dirt with a stick, and occasionally she reached down and picked up a stone and skipped it out across the river's current. But she couldn't buy into his excitement. The things that excited Bodo were intangible, and Fran wanted to *lay on hands*. She didn't want to *see* ocean liners, she wanted to be *on* one. She wanted to be *on* and *in* things, to *possess* them. And yet she listened, because something unexpected had begun to happen, and Bodo had tapped into a place in her she'd never suspected was there: beyond the excitement of the fast-paced life Bodo exposed her to — making love on drugs in a shotgun apartment on Bourbon Street with the air conditioner off and the French doors leading to the wrought iron balcony open and the sound of Dixieland coming in on the hot night's breeze from Preservation Hall around the corner — beyond all this, she felt tenderness toward him, tenderness and an impulse to protect him.

Still, she grew restless. The newness wore off and she became Bodo's girl, sitting at a back table night after night sipping free drinks. She could walk up and down the street and go into almost any club she wanted to without paying cover, and she could sit at any bar and drink at special prices. The routine of the Quarter began to reveal itself to her, the underlying desperation and the threadbare dreams, the ugly familiarity. She'd become part of the local color, what the tourists came to see, and every now and then, when this realization came over her, she became mildly alarmed. She began thinking about getting out.

She worked on Bodo for weeks with absolutely no results. He just shut down whenever she brought the subject up. "Go?" he'd say. "Go *where?*"

"Anywhere! Any goddamn place you want! Just let's get out of the Quarter. This place grows on you like fungus. It's fucking suffocating, baby. It's *evil.*"

"Evil?"

"If you won't come, I'll go without you," she said suddenly, and she knew immediately from his eyes that if it came down to it, he'd let her go.

It was Bert's card that turned the tide. "What's happening down in sump land?" Bert wanted to know. "Still selling peanuts to tourists and singing Bill Bailey twice a night? If you ever break free from that particular wheel of Samsara and want to spin on something with a bigger base, trip on out to San

Francisco and look me up." He signed it, and in the upper left corner, in a meticulous hand, he wrote a street address. Fran found the card on the night table beside the bed and went straight down into the club where Bodo was putting the chairs down, getting ready to open.

"Bodo, is this the Bert you're always talking about?"

"Sure is," Bodo said, continuing to put down chairs, but aware of the card in her hand.

"Well here's our chance!"

"Chance for what?"

"To get out! To move on! To go to San Francisco!"

"What for?"

"Jesus, Bodo! I'm serious. I've had it here."

He didn't answer, and suddenly she knew what she had to do. She knew it without thinking, it was one of those things women know beyond thinking so that later when you accuse them of it they don't know what you're talking about and are genuinely indignant.

"I'm going out there," she said. "I'll look up your friend and maybe he can get me headed in the right direction. I'm going alone if you won't come with me."

Bodo put one more chair down and then turned to face her. He still didn't say anything, but he began rocking slightly from foot to foot and a strange smile came over his face.

"We can get married!" Fran blurted out. "You can get back into broadcasting!" she said. She was giddy and saying anything that came into her head. She knew she had him and she was drunk with victory. And besides, she fancied the idea, being married to a DJ in a town like San Francisco. Things were on the move again. Things were looking up.

IV: San Francisco

They drove out of New Orleans in the MG, pulling the Honda behind in a U-Haul trailer. They took with them what they could carry and they took their time. They spent three days camped at the bottom of the Grand Canyon, and when they got to San Francisco, Bert put them up. He had a three-bedroom walk-up flat in the Sunset, wainscot walls and parquet floors. The room he gave them overlooked the street and had been set up as a writing room, but since he'd been working at the post office he didn't have the energy or concentration to devote to writing.

"Writing?" Bodo said.

They were sitting around the kitchen table, smoking a number and drinking beer. Bodo had already shredded the label off his bottle and now he was wadding it into small balls. As they drew closer to San Francisco, he'd become preoccupied thinking about Bert, preparing what he'd say to him. But now, sitting in Bert's kitchen, he was somehow stripped of all his preparation, and whatever he said went in through Bert's smile and boomeranged back at him.

"Just a porno novel," Bert said.

"*Porno!*" Bodo exclaimed.

"Sure," said Bert. "Why not?"

Nothing had changed. The burden was on Bodo to explain Bert's actions, and the silence that suddenly came over the table numbed his brain and emptied his mind of everything except the white winds of confusion. In that silence Bodo knew that they saw him as a fool. Once he had been Beau Bodo and bossed the Saturday morning airwaves, but now he was nothing. Only a week ago he had been naked in the sun with Fran at the bottom of the Grand Canyon, and now she sat at his side, looking down into her lap, embarrassed for him.

"I don't know," Bodo finally said. "Why not?"

"Precisely," said Bert, and Fran looked up from her lap and smiled at him.

* * *

Fran got a temporary job as a file clerk for an insurance firm. She and Bert left for work together, Bert dropping her off in his old Plymouth.

Bodo watched them leave each morning from the front room window, and as soon as the car rounded the corner, he turned and went straight to Bert's stash. He'd smoke a number sitting in the sunny kitchen with his chair tilted back and his bare feet resting on the green Formica table top, and then he'd get up and begin pacing the flat.

He got so he could tell the difference between various types of good grass. The mediocre stuff was all the same, but Panama Red and Acapulco Gold, for instance, had distinctively different effects on him. Gold went right to his head and produced thoughts by the millions, thoughts tripping all over themselves in their fresh excitement, and Red filled him with physical sensations and gave him a strong sense of earth, not the planet as a concept, but actual *earth* — rich, moist, and dark.

It was the Gold that he preferred. He'd toke up and then turn on the radio and enter into a dialogue with the KSAN DJs, plowing them under with his high-octane rap. Without talking with the DJs, Bodo felt like he existed in a cage. A yellow canary in his dark cage of solitude, the thin restraining ribs sloping down around his vibrating wings. At the end of the day, before Bert and Fran got home from work, he'd turn off the radio and clean up the apartment, open the windows to let in some fresh air, wash the dishes and take out the trash.

* * *

It went on like that for months. Each day Fran and Bert came home with work-world smells clinging to them. "What you been up to all day?" Bert invariably asked, and what could Bodo say?

He felt chopped off from everything. There was no continuity, no memory. He was furious with his lack of memory, he needed it to tie things together. Alone with the radio, he could string thoughts together, but when Bert and Fran came home, everything got confused. He couldn't relate to their thought patterns. What he said came out absurd when he was with them, and then he became desperate and began saying wild and frantic things in an attempt to compensate. They sucked all the energy from him with their certitude and left him smiling and rocking, spasms of pain shooting through his back, his neck aching and his head throbbing.

It was obvious they'd been talking about him behind his back. He could tell by the way they looked at each other, by the things they said to him. They were proof of something, the two of them, but what? Two positives made a minus, that's what. Keep the things that mean something to you separated from each other or they'll join forces and separate themselves from you.

* * *

They crossed Lincoln Avenue into Golden Gate Park and walked through the dark along the dirt trails. They passed shadows going in the other direction or sitting slumped on benches.

"What's wrong, hon?" Fran had asked him in bed the night before. She'd tried to arouse him, but he turned from her. "What is it, babe?" she said, but he would not answer. He was furious. He was frail and gentle and not built to contain such fury. He lay staring at the dark wall. In the distance, he could hear the foghorns. He felt her move away from him, turn on her side, and finding entry to sleep, leave him. The next morning she suggested the walk.

"Slow down," she said, trying to take his hand. "Your hand is cold as ice," she said.

"Yes dear," he said. "I know." He'd begun calling her dear.

They sat on a bench and Bodo searched his pockets for a long roach he'd brought with him.

"Don't light that now," she said, "I want to talk to you."

"So? Let's talk and smoke! Let's let our talk go up in smoke!" He was delighted that his words had come out so well.

"Hon, don't you think you should look for work?" she said.

"Hmmm," he said.

"I think you'll feel better if you do."

"I feel fine! Just fine!"

"Bodo, you can't just keep sitting around the house. It's not healthy. What do you do all day?"

"Read," he said. "Is there something wrong with that? I read, that's what." His voice was suddenly full of hostility, too much hostility, he thought — tone it down, get it right. A sensation came over him like a dark shadow moving over the ocean far out at sea, no one there to see it, just wind, sky, and ocean. He often got these sensations of being someplace in spirit where no living thing existed.

"No," she said. "There's nothing wrong with that." But she was backing off, she didn't mean what she said. "Let's light that roach now," she said.

He tried to light it, but his hands were trembling.

"Here," she said. "Let me." She took the roach from him and lit it with one swift strike of the match.

* * *

"What's going on?" Bodo said. It was two a.m. and he'd just come in the door from work. Bert smiled and took him by the arm, led him from the hallway into the living room. Ravi Shankar was on the stereo. The room was lit by candlelight. There were five or six of Bert's friends there, and Fran. Fran had landed a nursing job, and she was still in her uniform after getting off work. There was a big cake on a card table in the middle of the room with twenty-three candles on it. Fran came up to him and took his arm. Bert and Fran stood on either side of him, smiling, holding him by the arms.

The very next day after their talk in the park, Bodo had gone out and got work. He walked down Broadway in the bright sunlight and stopped under a green awning with the words *Hoosier Stick* painted on it in bright yellow letters. A set of double doors were hooked open with tarp straps, and he stuck his head inside the dark club and waited for his eyes to adjust. There was the smell of stale beer, and then he made out the familiar outline of chairs piled on table tops. He walked inside the club and across the sawdust floor to a long bar with a brass foot rail and tall stools on the customer side. Behind the bar a Chinaman in a red vest was unpacking a box of new beer mugs.

"I've come about the job," Bodo said.

"Can you clap?" the Chinaman asked, and looked up from his work with an inscrutable smile.

"It's a surprise!" Fran said. "Isn't it nice?"

"Surprise?" said Bodo.

"It's my birthday, silly!" she said.

"Your birthday?"

"Yes! And *you* forgot all about it. Bert found out and gave me this surprise party."

"No big deal," Bert said. "Just something spontaneous that popped into my head this afternoon. I tried to get hold of you to help plan it, but you weren't at home."

It was true. He'd been out cruising on the Honda.

"It's a real special party," Bert said, and he held out his hand. There was a pill in it. They were all on mescaline.

" . . . It's only through violence, don't you see, that we can make the actual course of human or other physical events fit our description of them . . . "

" . . . the *mind*, you must realize, functions on a linear plane, whereas the *brain* is multi-dimensional . . . "

" . . . the problem is that the ego sees itself as the captain of the ship, whereas it is only a small part of our bodies and minds which in turn are part and parcel of a great cosmic energy system which — much as a peach tree bears peaches — bears people. And violence, therefore, I would think . . . "

Bodo sat staring at his hands. He looked at them and they didn't turn into blobs or begin running away like water as he'd thought they might, but they had taken on a *presence* that was totally new. Or ancient. Yes, uralt. *Uralt?*

"You people talk too much," Bodo said, and he silenced the room. "You're just jackin' off your minds," he said.

"Oh, man," someone said. "Do we have to listen to this?"

"Hey, Bodo," Bert said from across the room. "Be cool, man."

Fran put her hand on his arm. "Bodo?" she said.

He looked at her and she was a total stranger. He was astounded that they'd been living together for a half year. She was the only person he'd ever lived with that closely, and now here she was, giving off stranger readings. He thought of Dardanelle and that one night with her, and that one night seemed to outdistance all the time he'd been with Fran. Then a series of realizations washed over him, memory flashes mixed with fantasy, his father holding out solace to him in the kitchen while on the verge of dying, his grandfather with his shoes off on the lush grass of the nursing home, and a shot of something else — standing in a strange basement in splendid isolation. Then something vague, the faces of many children looking down at him, a big man sweeping him up into his arms . . .

The images stopped there. Beyond lay an expanse of loneliness and terror that even under the influence of the mescaline his mind recoiled from. A shudder ran through Bodo, and his eyes, which had closed when the images started, opened.

Fran took her hand from his arm when she saw the look on his face. She began shaking her head as if denying something, and then Bert was there, squeezing in between them, putting an assuring arm around each of them.

"Hey, don't you guys get weird now," he said. "Try to relax. Flow with it. Trust it. These are all good people here. Don't get paranoid, okay?"

Fran took a deep breath, exhaled, and leaned her head on Bert's shoulder. Bert withdrew his arm from around Bodo's shoulder to better comfort her, and Bodo got up and went into the kitchen.

Bodo took a quart bottle of Coke from the refrigerator, opened it, and went back to stand in the doorway of the living room. The conversation had picked up again. They were trying to figure out how to pull out of Samsara and wondering if Krishnamurti and his totally informal, intuitive approach could really work in our structured, modern world.

Bodo stared at Fran across the room. She was talking with Bert and studiously avoiding him where he stood in the doorway. Everyone was doing it, establishing a flight pattern for their eyes that did not have to cross the doorway. It was difficult, and when their glances did stray to the vicinity of the door, they lowered their eyes to run the glance along the floor, at Bodo's feet. He watched this going on with an expanding fascination, and finally he laughed. He threw his head back and laughed, and again the room grew quiet; they all stared at him.

"Do you think space is an amniotic fluid?" he said, and when no one answered he laughed again, turned, and went clattering down the stairs to the Honda.

* * *

The three of them sat around the kitchen table, the sun streaming in over the green Formica. Bodo hadn't been to sleep for nearly seventy-two hours, since the night of the party. He'd been busy cleaning up the city, first filling gunnysacks with trash from the beaches along The Great Highway, and then moving on to North Beach where the police finally picked him up.

"Bodo, you're a genuine crazy man," Bert said, chuckling and shaking his head.

"It's time someone did something," Bodo said.

"Damn right, but listen, old buddy, listen to what I'm telling you. This is very complex business."

"You always told me it was pretty simple. Truth is simplicity, that's what you used to say in New Orleans."

"Well, and it is, too . . . " Bert trailed off, shook a cigarette from a pack, and lit it. He squinted critically but not unkindly at Bodo. It was a look calculated to bring Bodo under his wing, and as he gave it, he was acutely aware of Fran studying him.

"Man, you look terrible, you know that? You looked at yourself in a mirror lately?"

Bodo laughed — a jerky, agitated laugh. "Sure!" he said, "the mirrors of small children's faces! They all smile back at me!"

Bert shook his head as if Bodo was missing the point. "You know the difference between simplicity and simplistic?" he asked.

"Sure!" Bodo said, but he wasn't sure.

"Uh-huh," Bert said. "Well, you certainly aren't acting like it. What you're acting like is simplistic, which isn't such a hot thing. Just because you get a little overwhelmed by things, man, you can't go around trying to fit the entire world into your own personal idea of how it *should* be. *That* is simplistic, not simplicity. *Simplicity* comes from understanding the *complexity* of life, and if you can't handle that paradox, then you've got a ways to go."

Bodo's mind was emptying fast. Exhaustion was bringing him to his knees. Exhaustion and Bert again, Bert was tucking him away for a good night's sleep.

Bodo fought to keep his eyes brilliant and invincible. He shook his head and looked down at the sun on the Formica and could think of nothing to say. He felt Fran's eyes on him, sensed her looking back and forth from him to Bert as they talked.

"You listening?" Bert was saying. "Here, take this." He handed Bodo a pill.

Bodo rolled it around between his street-dirty fingers, and as he did so, the last vestige of resistance died in him and he washed it down with coffee.

"Take a shower and hit the sack," Bert told him. "You'll sleep like a baby."

* * *

Bodo'd wait for Fran and Bert to leave for work in the morning, and then he'd cruise the streets on the Honda. He'd lost the MG. Two of the tires had gone flat, and a cluster of parking tickets had accumulated on the windshield, topped, finally, with a fluorescent notice that said the car would be towed away, and then one day it was gone.

He spent a lot of time in Golden Gate Park, playing ball with groups of children, and sometimes he'd go to an all-black bar on Haight Street. He was the only white male who went there. He'd sit at the bar drinking whisky and try to engage people in conversation. Once he tried to get a black woman to leave with him, and the bartender took a bar towel and began studiously cleaning the bar directly in front of him, leaning into the bar towel and telling Bodo in a low voice, "Man, you are not being cool. It's fine with me if you want to come here, but you best be cool, you understand?"

And Bodo did understand, he was filled with joy at having a message float into his mind so unequivocally, and he told the bartender so, he told him how people are sealed off in cages with their wings pressed to their sides, how we are all kept from flight by some invisible, unbearable oppression, and how wonderful it is when someone is capable of expressing love in a simple way — not a simplistic way, you understand, but a simple way — and how he could relax here in this bar with these quiet, dark people, how the rest of his world was bright and loud . . .

The bartender stopped wiping the bar and stared at Bodo, the woman he had asked to leave with him frowned into her drink, and all the men up and down the bar stared with silent perfection straight ahead into the gloom.

Bodo felt no danger. He knew this was one of his homes. He began to see that life had many homes, and that the task is to seek out those places where you can rest your head.

He went out into the bright day and walked down Haight Street. The windows were boarded up, and debris lay collected in the gutters. The Love Children were no longer there, but obstinate spare-changers with bad skin and hepatitis eyes still slouched in the doorways, and looking at them, Bodo became filled with determination. Flower boxes. It would take flower boxes. Flower boxes and trees right in the middle of intersections, that would be the first step in bringing beauty back into life. And it would be practical, too, it would work better than stop signs and could be accomplished in no time at all — crews with jackhammers could break up the pavement and blacktop throughout the city, and Forest Rangers could tag along after them and put in the trees.

He was on mescaline again. He'd gone into Bert's stash and helped himself to three hits, and this time he wouldn't wear down, this time he'd keep the fire of determination stoked until the job was done.

When Bert got home from work, there was a pile of mahogany one-by-eights on the sidewalk and Bodo was trying to bang nails into the mortar between the building bricks. Red chips lay on the sidewalk all around him.

"What the hell are you *doing?*" Bert asked.

"Flowers!" Bodo said. "We need flowers!"

Bert reached out and snatched the hammer from Bodo's hand. "You goddamn fool," he said. "You want to go crazy, go find a flat of your own to do it in. Take your own consequences. I'm getting a little tired of this weird shit you've been layin' down around here."

"Weird shit?" Bodo said, an intense, lunatic grin all over his face. "What weird shit?"

When Fran came home Bert met her on the landing. Bodo could hear their lowered voices. And then she came into the room where he was sitting on the bed in the dark. She sat beside him and shared the grass he was smoking, and then she stood up and slowly slipped out of her uniform and wiped the slate of his mind clean of madness with the movement of her body.

*　*　*

They moved to a place on Parnassus in the Haight, and Bert thought he'd seen the last of them. It was just as well. There was a thing between him and Fran that he was reluctant to let go of, but he was a survivor and he could let go of anything. He'd finish the porno novel, sell it for quick cash, and then split for Hawaii. He knew some people over there on one of the smaller islands who had land and were living a laid-back existence, growing dynamite weed and selling it on the mainland. He'd been in San Francisco throughout the early sixties, right up to the Summer of Love in '67, after which he split for New Orleans. He'd seen it come and go, and being back in San Francisco, in his quieter moments, filled him with sadness.

It was all rip-off now. The Switchboard was gone, the Free Clinic and the Hip Job Co-op were gone, everything was gone. Up in smoke. In vapor. Burned out and boarded up. No beatific highs on Sandoz and Owsley acid, just a lot of wasted, leftover souls pushing their self-determined deadline of thirty, geezing and brown-bagging away what was left of their high-powered dreams. The smart ones had left a long time ago. The Grateful Dead packed up and left before the Summer of Love had run its course, recognizing for the end what every media outlet in the country was hyping as the beginning. Places like Morningstar Ranch were beginning to coalesce and the movement back to the land was underway.

The love scene had been a lot of fool's gold flashing under a San Francisco sun. And then the fog rolled in. And the narcs remembered what they were there for. And the dope turned bad and expensive and *basically* what happened is the energy gave out. Kesey was off resting on a rural route close to his childhood, girding himself for middle age; Leary had turned political; Dr. HIPpocrates switched his column from the *Berkeley Barb* to the *Chronicle,* the shows at the Fillmore were being priced out of reach, and everyone had the clap. The Hare Krishna people still went swarming down the streets in their flashy saffron robes, chanting and banging their tambourines, but no one now was curious enough to stop and stare. The world went by in a straight line, head down and hands in pockets.

It was over. Bert had known it back in '67, and so he got out. A lot of people he knew didn't and paid for their mistake with disillusionment or by doing time on a bust or their lives. The ones who got out either melted back into the mainstream or moved to islands in the middle of vast ideological oceans. And that's where Bert was going. He knew the back-to-the-land idea would also run its course, but it was still a young concept and it would take time for the energy drags to start hanging around, time for the media to focus its lens. He'd go to Hawaii and he'd —

The buzzer sounded and Bert got up from the chair he'd been daydreaming in and went to the window, pulled the drape back a fraction of an inch, and looked down into the street. Bodo was looking back at him from the sidewalk, his hand shading his eyes against the sun, leaning against a brand new Cadillac El Dorado. It was over a month since Bert had seen him. He was barefoot and wore dirty jeans and a grey sweat-shirt. His hair was uncombed and scraggly, and he'd let the fuzz grow out on his face. He was grinning up at the apartment, and the moment he saw the drapes move, his hand came away from his eyes, forming a fist with the index finger pointing. Bert let go of the drape and went down to open the door.

He wouldn't sit down. He had a leather pouch tied to a belt loop on his jeans with thick string. The pouch was full of dope. He emptied it on the table, selected a pill, and swallowed it. "Want some?" he asked Bert. Bert declined.

"Why do you always bring me into the kitchen?" Bodo asked. "You always try to sit me down at the kitchen table."

"I do?" Bert said.

"Yep. Sure do. But I'm not sitting down today. Uh-uh. Hey! Sun, Fun and *Kids!*"

"What are you on?" Bert asked.

"Huh. What aren't you on? That's the question."

Bert felt suddenly very tired. "That your car down there?" he asked.

"Nope," Bodo said. "Belongs to some lady."

"What lady?"

"Who knows! Who cares! Sun, Fun and *Kids!*"

"Sun, fun and kids, huh?"

"Yep! Getting younger all the time!"

"Where'd you get the car, Bodo?"

"Lady gave it to me!"

"*Gave* it to you? A Cadillac El Dorado?"

"Yep!"

"Well lucky you."

"Told me to drive it around for her. Told me to *enjoy!* She was in the store buying cigarettes, about to cry because she had an appointment at the hospital across the street and she couldn't find a place to park her car. So I told her I'd drive it around and pick her up in two hours. Hey!"

"She gave you the keys?"

"Yep!"

Bert shrugged. He went into the bathroom and took a piss, and after that he went into the bedroom and called Fran. By the time she arrived, Bodo had already left to return the car.

"What do you think?" Bert asked. He was glad to see her again.

She lit a cigarette, exhaled the smoke, and then rested her head in her hands, her elbows on the table. "Jesus, I don't know what to think. It's like living in an insane asylum. I can't get through to him anymore. I think I'd leave him, but I'm afraid of what he might do."

"You think he's dangerous?"

"Not to me, to himself. I don't know what he'd do to himself. He's so different than when I met him. He used to be fun and crazy, but crazy in a good way. This thing now — there's no contact. I mean *no* contact. It scares me. I don't know how it all got started. I feel like I've aged ten years."

Bert leaned over and took her hand. She pulled her hand away, shook her head, and took another drag on her cigarette. He leaned back in his chair and lit a cigarette of his own.

"He hardly ever sleeps anymore," she said. "He goes until he passes out and then he has dreams, real bad dreams. He mutters sounds that don't make any sense, like he's talking in tongues, and then he starts thrashing around and I have to get out of the bed, get out of his way. I stand by the bed and yell at him — 'Bodo! Bodo!' — over and over again. I'm afraid to grab hold of him, I don't know if he'll wake up, like he might grab hold of me while he's still in the dream, think he's got hold of whatever it is in the dream and do something to me. You know?"

Bert shook his head.

"And Jesus, he smokes dope *all* the time. And he takes pills, I'm never sure what he's on, he's always popping something into his mouth and there's no way to tell what's affecting him."

"You thought of getting help?"

"Psychiatric help?"

"Yes."

"I'm a nurse. I've seen enough of that. They'll just turn off his ignition with Thorazine or something."

"Maybe counseling of some kind. Get him to a crisis center, a therapy session, someplace where he could compare notes with people like himself."

"People like himself?" Fran said.

Bert shrugged his shoulders. He offered her a ride home.

At Fran's place they made sandwiches and washed them down with beer. They sat in front of the bay window and smoked some of Bert's Hawaiian, and gradually it got dark. They sat in the dark across from each other, not saying much, watching the lights come on in the houses that sloped away from Fran's fourth-story apartment. It was like watching hundreds of campfires being started, the campfires of some massive, conquering army, thousands of years before the birth of Christ. They had vivid images of the warriors who sat around the campfires preparing their gear and their weapons for the next day's battle; large, thick-boned men, so sturdy as to be almost of another species. They could feel the sharp chill of the pre-Christian night, see the breath of the tethered horses, silver in the blackness, and feel the sharp lust of that primitive time. They stared into the darkness between them and felt the instant understanding that they'd shared from the first time they met. Then they heard it, the roar of the bike, gearing down around a corner and then speed-shifting smartly on the climb, and they both knew it wasn't Bodo driving. They didn't get up to look out the window. They heard the bike pull up to the curb, heard voices, and then the bike roared off again, speed shifting and diminishing into the darkness. Next there was the sound of a key searching for the door lock, and Fran got up and crossed the room, turning on a table lamp as she passed it, straightening her clothes and brushing her hair back before opening the door.

He was dead drunk. He had vomit down the front of his shirt and had pissed his pants. He could barely stand upright. Between them they got him to the couch.

"Should we wash him up?" Bert asked. "Put him in the shower?"

"No," she said. "Just let him lay there. Let him sleep it off. Jesus."

Suddenly he sat up, his eyes glazed. "Sun, Fun and Kids!" he said, the battered grin working its way into the lines of his face. "Sun, Fun . . . " and he began to fade.

Fran grabbed him by the shoulders and began shaking him violently. "Where's your bike, Bodo? What did you do with your bike? *Do you hear me?*"

His eyes opened again and he shrank back from her, wrapping his arms around his head and pulling his legs up.

"Bodo!" she said, her fury turned to grief. "Oh Jesus, goddamn you!"

"Bodo," he said, from deep down in his unconsciousness, "Bodo . . . " But he said it with a strange accent, and it was not the name she knew so well.

* * *

The Honda was parked on the sidewalk, leaning against the building. He had to lean it because it had no kickstand — he'd taken it off when he hammered in the dents.

Bert and Fran told him he was a fool the day after he'd come in so drunk, a fool for letting a total stranger ride off on his bike. They told him he'd gone and lost his bike, and when was he going to open his eyes and snap out of this thing? Bodo grinned. It was unnerving how he could wake up after such a drunk and pick up again *right where he'd left off.* Light up a number, eat an apple, pop a pill, and start right in.

"Sun, Fun and Kids!" he said. "He'll bring it back."

"*Who?*" said Bert. "*Who'll* bring it back?"

They'd decided the night before, after seeing Bodo like that, after hearing the strange voices in him, that they'd have to get tough.

"My friend," Bodo said. "He'll bring the bike back."

"Sure he will," Bert said. "Jesus, Bodo, snap out of it! *Listen* to me, goddamn it. You're losing it, man. I mean really *losing* it. Just take a look at yourself. Go in the bathroom and look in the mirror. Man, you have to stop taking drugs. We'll help. We'll do everything we can. But you've got to start the ball rolling. You're not in touch with reality anymore."

"Reality?" Bodo said, and then they heard the Honda coming up the hill.

They sat there with the morning sun streaming through the bay window and listened. The bike pulled up outside and the engine went dead. A few moments later there was a knock on the door. Fran opened it.

"I'm looking for a guy who owns a Honda. I forgot the dude's name, but he's righteous, and he gave me this apartment number."

Fran stood back and the man stepped uneasily into the room. He was big and rough looking, dressed in faded jeans, biker boots, and an expensive sheepskin jacket. He saw Bodo sitting on the couch and went over to him. His uneasiness disappeared.

"There ya are!" he said. "Hey, man! She took me back! All that shit you ran down last night — it worked. I said it and it worked! Too fucking much, man!"

"Sun, Fun and *Kids!*" Bodo said. "Getting younger all the time!"

"Yeah!" the man said. "Goddamn right!" And then, to Fran and Bert, "This cat just laid his bike on me." He returned his attention to Bodo. He frowned and shook his head, as if he'd been weighing something and had come to a conclusion. He slipped off his sheepskin jacket and laid it across Bodo's lap.

"Back to Year One!" Bodo said.

"That's right, pardner," the man said. "You keep tellin' it like it is." He turned and left the apartment without another word.

They insisted it was a fluke that a total stranger had returned his bike, and that no one in his right mind gives away a $200 jacket.

"Only crazy people give gifts?" Bodo said.

But he did not want them to be unhappy, he wanted them to be filled with love as he wanted the entire world to be filled with love, and he went downstairs that very afternoon after Bert had left and put in the dents.

Fran came running out into the street in alarm. "What are you doing? What are you doing?" she screamed, and then, in a more subdued tone, noticing the crowd that had begun to gather, "Bodo, please come upstairs. Give me the hammer and come upstairs."

"But dear," he said. "I'm doing this for you. To make you happy! Don't you see? I don't want you to worry about my bike getting stolen, so I'm putting in these dents. No one will rip off such an ugly thing, dear! And it will run as good as ever!"

The crowd murmured. "He's got a point there, lady," a mailman said, and Fran stormed back into the building.

When he'd finished with the dents he took off the kickstand to make the bike even less attractive, and then he removed both rearview mirrors for a more complicated reason. He was going back to the Year One, but he was going forward to get there. Mirrors are reflections of the past, he reasoned, and the past is all wrong.

That afternoon, after Fran left for work, he painted all the mirrors in the house black. When she returned from work she was furious about the bathroom and bedroom mirrors, but when she opened the top drawer to her vanity the next morning and found the small pocket mirror shrouded in black, she felt a fear more deeply rooted and inexplicable than any she'd ever experienced in her life.

* * *

Bodo's continually worsening appearance did not work in his favor at the Hoosier Stick, but the night he started giving away drinks and tipping customers with his bank money, the Chinaman called him aside and handed him a check he'd written on the spot. "That squares us," he told Bodo, smiling his inscrutable smile.

It was alright with Bodo. It gave him time to concentrate on more important things. Like the children. If he could only get to the children before it was too late. Start the children back to the Year One before the road grew too long. Make them happy. Christmas was just around the corner, and there wasn't a moment to lose.

He drove the Honda to the Drogstore on the corner of Haight and Ashbury. He placed the small, artificial Christmas tree on its stand in the middle of the intersection, took out a roll of one-dollar bills, and fastened them to the tree with paper clips. The children would come now. The children of the Haight who had seen magic go threadbare. They would be filled with awe and amazement. Magic would be renewed in them, and the magic would spawn love. Love and magic spring from the same *uralt* fountain. He'd looked the word up. There were forces working inside him, putting words into his vocabulary before he knew their meaning. He went into the Drogstore and got a cup of espresso. It cost two dollars. He paid the waitress with two singles and tipped her another. She smiled and told him to have a good trip. Then she drifted off.

They were all frightened, but he'd deal with their fear, he'd hunt it down. His mind was working better now. Things were connecting. He was going to smash the recalcitrant past to smithereens. He was tapped into the rhythms of the universe. He settled down at his small table next to the window and watched his tree, its money leaves blowing gently in the ocean breeze coming up through Golden Gate Park. He waited for the children.

They came slowly, hesitantly. They gathered on one corner with their hands in their pockets and watched the traffic swerve around the tree. Some spare-changers mixed in with the children. Darkness came, and once there was almost an accident caused by a car swerving to miss the Money Tree. Then the first child made her move. She sprinted out into the intersection and grabbed several dollar bills, then sprinted back to the other children. They examined the money, and then the intersection was filled with children, tearing at the tree, a few spare-changers slapping the children aside while horns bleated, traffic jammed, and spectators gathered.

* * *

Bodo was disappointed with the way things turned out with the Money Tree. What was needed was a bigger tree. He rode into Golden Gate Park and noticed the gigantic pine. What was it? A ponderosa? They were in the process of decorating it. The Power Company was going to string a million lights on the tree and then fill them with electricity. It was a futile gesture. It was a cold, electric gesture. It did not help the children. The poor children with empty bellies and no toys would stand in the cold night and look at the cold tree and nothing would be gained. Bodo stopped at the first phone booth he came to and thumbed through the pages until he found what he thought was the right number. It wasn't. He was referred to another number and then another until he ran out of dimes. He got on his bike and rode to the Power Building. He'd handle the matter face-to-face with the Head of Power. He'd explain the futility of stringing so many lights on such a large tree. He'd suggest that instead the Power Company spend the money and the energy in supplying the poor children with gifts. Send trucks through the streets with people in the back tossing gifts this way and that.

Bodo paced back and forth on the thick carpet in front of the big desk. The man behind the desk leaned back in his chair and listened. He watched Bodo pacing. He saw his obsession and admired his conviction and his guts; ignored his appearance and said: "Alright, young man, you have a good point. I'll tell you what I'll do. We have to decorate the tree, we do it every year and people have come to expect it. Some people even *depend* on it. I think you'll find it is a joy to the old. And old folks have a place in life as well as children, don't you think?"

Bodo had stopped pacing. He shook his head in agreement. He'd not yet mentioned the Year One to the Head of Power. He'd not mentioned Sun, Fun and Kids. Or talked about mirrors. He'd avoided these things. He'd spoken in more conventional concepts, and he was about to get what he came for. But something stirred in him, some beast that he'd been out to slay, some tension and pain. He shook his head in agreement with what the Head of Power said. The Head of Power smiled. He saw Bodo falter. He knew he would. He was young. But the Head of Power would give him a little encouragement, because it was Christmas.

"Yes, of course. I knew you'd understand. You're an intelligent and sensitive young man, I can see that. And so I'm going to grant your request. We'll decorate the tree *and* give gifts to the children."

Bodo smiled. "Thank you," he said. He stood in front of the desk with his hands folded in front of him.

The Head of Power smiled again and came up out of his chair. He was a big man. He came around from behind the desk and placed a hand on Bodo's shoulder. He walked him to the door like a father. At the door he shook his hand and then the door closed silently behind him and Bodo was left in a large room full of secretaries and clerks. He turned to face them.

He walked the long walk between their desks and their office machines to the corridor door. Going down in the elevator, he popped some speed-laced purple-dome acid. Street drugs were turning nasty. You never knew what you were getting. Bodo had never heard of Sandoz acid. He did not know who Augustus Owsley Stanley III was. He did not know that he was walking through the aftermath of the greatest dream America had ever had. He rode home and began painting the walls of the apartment with signs and symbols of his own choosing.

* * *

It was right there in the paper for all to see. Bodo told them what he'd done and they didn't believe him, but then Bert saw it while reading the Sunday paper in bed, Bodo's story being covered by one of the top columnists in the city. A young man with the true spirit of Christmas had practically forced himself into the office of the Head of Power to plead the case of the poor children. His plea had been heard and the Power Company was going to set up Food and Gift Distribution Centers in the Fillmore, the Mission, and at Hunter's Point where the children could line up for free gifts and hot turkey on paper plates.

Bert brought the paper by the apartment. Fran was there alone. The walls were a mess, covered by strange drawings and cryptic messages. Fran threw up her hands. "There goes our cleaning deposit," she said. He showed her the paper, a red circle around the article about Bodo. She read it sitting at the kitchen table. "Jesus Christ," she said. "Can you believe it? How long can he keep on like this? This can't go on."

Bert stood behind her chair. She'd slept late and was still in her negligee. He could see her breasts through the diaphanous material. He bent over her from behind and cupped her breasts. She arched her back, pushing her breasts into his hands, leaning her head back with her eyes closed. He began running his lips lightly over the fine hairs on the back of her neck, moving the hair with the warmth of his breath. She placed her hands over his on her breasts and they began to move together.

* * *

Bodo is suddenly surrounded by motorcycles. He is at a streetlight on Broadway, heading toward the freeway entrance. The bikers rev their machines and drown out the puny sound of his Honda. Bodo is delighted. He revs his Honda for all it's worth. He grins around him at the bikers. They look at him deadpan. Then one of them smiles slightly and gives him the power sign. Bodo returns the salute, and when the light changes, the bikers roar through the Broadway Tunnel and onto the freeway. Bodo crosses the Bay Bridge surrounded by Hell's Angels.

* * *

She no longer slept with him. Not only had he stopped brushing his teeth and combing his hair, but he seldom bathed. He smelled of dry, sour sweat. She began sleeping at Bert's.

Bert had given up on his porno novel and quit the post office. He was fronting grass for the people in Hawaii, selling in quantity to smaller dealers, planning to make a lot of money fast and then get out, buy some land in the mountains, play his cards right and never have to work again. Maybe he'd take Fran with him. Maybe he'd marry her and raise a family. He wasn't getting any younger. And she wasn't getting any younger, either. No one was getting any younger, no matter what Bodo said.

Bert wished that things would come to a head in Bodo. As long as things went on like this, there was no breaking free of him. When all was said and done, Bodo made him feel banal. Banal? Frivolous. At times even hypocritical. At times? Made him hear his own voice. Let's face it, he was fucking Bodo's old lady, and Bodo's old lady was the best fuck he'd ever had. Bodo was a fool to let her go in order to chase sparks of truth through the night sky.

But it was because of Bodo that it worked between them. Bodo's innocence and ignorance highlighted Bert's baseness, and it was this baseness that Fran made love to. There were no illusions between them, and when they fucked, they engaged in a brutal honesty. Take Bodo out of the equation, and the whole thing would go flat. They'd get married and live in the mountains in the memory of these days. They'd fuck other people for cheap thrills and always come back together, united forever in the base honesty that Bodo made possible.

* * *

The apartment on Parnassus was a pigsty. The garbage hadn't been taken out in months. The toilet was flushed only when Fran or Bert stopped by, and dirty dishes were piled everywhere. The floors of all the rooms were covered with the unbelievable variety of things Bodo brought home with him. There were trails that wound through it all, connecting strategic spots like the toilet, the bed, and the front door.

The walls were covered with primitive paintings and chalk drawings. An orange, smiling sun covered one entire wall, and there was an abundance of gnarled, stark black trees that the sun seemed unable to nourish. There were rivers and ponds along which stood preoccupied rabbits and birds. There were no people. Over the door were the words: THE MASCULINE EARTH WRITERS. No one knew what it meant. There were other things like:

KNOW HOW TO OPERATE YOUR BRAIN METABOLISM!

THE HAPPY MEDIAN AGE FOR LIVING FOREVER IS 23!

THE UNIVERSAL SECRET WILL NOW BE DISCLOSED TO THE WHOLE WORLD — YOU BETTER COVER UP YOUR MIRRORS, OR ELSE IT'LL BE CURTAINS FOR YOU.

And longer things like:

Take all the words and either spell them backwards or doctor the word up and insert it into fresh, clean, healthy words.

For instance, the word raw. Now that spelled backwards still spells raw, right? Or it can *Run Around Willow.* Or better yet, maybe you'll recognize it here — *Women Are Remembrance.*

Some other words you'll recognize: 1) dab. 2) dlo. 3) dloc. 4) etah. 5) llik. 6) truh. 7) ton. 8) on.

Remember now: nature plus children plus art plus music! *Sun-Fun-Kids,* the *San Francisco Kingdom!*

Bert and Fran walked through the debris of Bodo's life on Good Friday. They picked things up and let them fall again, like tourists in a novelty shop. They stood before the drawings and words on the walls with their hands at their sides, not quite sure where to pigeonhole what they were seeing. They'd come to bring Bodo away with them for the weekend. They were going to take him into the mountains to a monastery to witness a sunrise Mass, to show him that mystery and truth can indeed function hand-in-hand with established order. It was another of their perfunctory attempts to lend a hand. It was part of the ritual they were ensnared in. That's what Bodo might have told them if he'd been there — they were all ensnared in ritual. But he wasn't.

"Jesus," Fran said. "Open a window. This place reeks." Bert pulled the drapes and a cloud of dust went up. He opened a window and the sweet spring air entered the room. Fran walked resolutely into the kitchen and rolled up her sleeves. She tackled the dishes. "Let's clean this place up," she said.

"Sure," said Bert. "Good idea."

"Take the trash down, will you? And drive over to that hardware store on Judah and get some paint remover and whitewash. Let's clean up these mirrors and walls."

"Okay," Bert said. He gathered up several bags of garbage and went down the elevator with them.

While Bert and Fran worked on the apartment, Bodo was attending a pagan ritual down at the Family Dog on the Great Highway. Just the names of the places on the flier in the Blue Unicorn were enough to draw him there: Family Dog, Great Highway — magic names.

The Family Dog was smack dab in the middle of an amusement park, which Bodo found amusing and just as it should be. More and more he was seeing the inevitable order in things. There was no way to make chaos of it. He moved around now in an almost constant state of ecstasy. He saw the crux of every second that passed. He was approaching the gravitational pull of the Year One.

The Family Dog was a place where rock concerts had been held in the '60s, before the whole thing got too big for a cozy place like the Dog to contain. Bands like the Grateful Dead had played there. The Mothers of Invention. Big Brother and the Holding Company. But now the Dog lay quiet most of the time amidst the twirling rides, the thundering roller-coaster, the squeals and laughs and screams of everyday people.

Salvo G, a latter-day prophet, held religious meetings at the Dog. It was just the right size for his following of about 800. Men and women in their late twenties, for the most part, sitting on the floor with their children and chanting *Om* until Salvo G felt the right vibe; then he'd close his eyes, take a deep breath and hold it, sit up there on his modestly raised platform on a cushion in the full lotus with his hands on his knees palms out, his index fingers and thumbs making little circles; eventually he'd open his eyes and look peacefully around him, smiling. His followers relaxed, smiled back, murmurs of joy rippling through their ranks. These were the same people who only a few short years earlier had been writhing under the strobes to an insane decibel onslaught in the very same space.

"Same space, different time!" Bodo said from the back of the room.

Salvo G's method was to lecture on whatever aspect of his brand of World View that seemed appropriate for the night, and then to field questions from the floor. He'd given the nod to Bodo, and instead of addressing himself to the karma of Good Friday that was heavy upon them all, Bodo drew a parallel between the Then and the Now.

"Five or six years ago you were dancing and making the timbers shiver, and now you're all exhausted and sitting cross-legged and collapsed like cows — *on the very same floor!* You've given up the music!"

Heads were turning. Salvo G made a clucking sound with his tongue against the roof of his mouth and shook his own head sadly. He cleared his throat.

"Things evolve," said Salvo G . . .

"Things are as they should be!" said Bodo.

"Things evolve according to . . . "

"Things are heading straight back to *Year One!*" said Bodo.

"If you have a question, friend, I'll do my best to answer it, but —"

"Sun, Fun and *Kids!*" said Bodo. "The San Francisco Kingdom!"

On Easter Sunday morning, Salvo G and the hardcore of his flock were up in Sutro Park overlooking the Pacific Ocean. They stood together as a family, awaiting the sun. The sun would rise in the east and cast its golden light over the endless swell of the dark ocean, driving back the shadow, and the ocean would come alive. The ceremony would begin. No one knew what the ceremony would be, Salvo G made it up as he went along, but it would begin. They waited.

Bodo came out of the bushes behind them. He'd been riding around on his Honda for several weeks now, his sleeping bag strapped down behind him, sleeping wherever he pleased. When he was hungry he went out behind grocery stores and bakeries and found marvelous things in Dempsey Dumpsters. Or he'd simply knock on a door and announce his hunger, and people fed him. For the past two nights, though, he'd been sleeping in the park. He'd left Salvo G's meeting on Good Friday and wandered up there. He felt at home in the park. Protected. Each night at midnight and again at three in the morning, a patrol car cruised through, its spotlight searching for anyone who might wish Bodo harm. Bodo smiled as they drove through and whispered his thanks. And now he had guests. Salvo G had brought some of his following to celebrate Easter Sunday. The Resurrection. The Year One.

Bodo walked up to the back of the group. He was rocking and grinning. He put his arm around a man's waist and gave him a brotherly squeeze. The man looked at him uneasily and smiled faintly. Bodo nodded and grinned, rocked and kept silent, an index finger hatch-marked across his lips.

Then the light of the sun fanned out over the ocean, throwing back the darkness, and Salvo G stretched his long, imposing form toward the heavens, his hands trembling in the golden morning, his head back and his eyes closed. A murmur of amazement rippled through the gathering as the black ocean turned golden before their eyes.

"The son of God has risen and pushed the darkness from the earth!" Salvo G intoned. "All praise the Lord!"

"Amen!" Bodo responded in a loud, cheery voice. "Amen, brother!"

"Amen," said a few of the following, but hesitantly — amen was not something they usually said.

"Let us join hands in this moment of revelation, let us feel the love of Christ flow through us!" said Salvo G, and he turned from the ocean, scanning faces for the intruder.

Before he could spot him, the group joined hands in a large circle and began singing a song written for the occasion by one of the women. Bodo got out the D harp that he'd bought only a week earlier from a black kid in the Fillmore, and he ducked into the circle. He began dancing and playing the harp.

The singing came to a halt. The group continued holding hands, but their arms hung limp. Salvo G stepped into the circle with Bodo.

"You'll have to leave," he said, standing spread-eagle. "You're disturbing our worship." Salvo G wore a flowing white robe with a black sash. Bodo wore the same pair of jeans he'd had on for the past three weeks, the sheepskin jacket (now filthy and with a large rip in the sleeve), and Vietnam jungle boots.

"Sun, Fun and *Kids!*" Bodo said. "God is love! Dog is God! Easter is the symbol of the Year One! We're all getting younger!"

"I said you'll have to leave, friend. You're laying your trip on everyone. You're ripping off the communal energy."

"How can that be?" Bodo said, rocking now, not dancing. "Where would I put it? There's no room! Energy fills up every last bit of space! It's *all* communal!"

The hands began to disengage and the circle began to lose form.

"Friend, if you wish to join us, you're welcome. But you must be peaceable."

"You just don't want me to sing and dance. This is the same old trip. One guy lording it over everyone else. Let's all take off our clothes! Let's take off our clothes and dance on the beach! Swim for Jesus! Let's frolic in the sand! Let's — "

"Be gone, Satan!" Salvo G thundered, cutting Bodo off in mid-sentence, startling him with the power of his voice. "We will not engage in violence," Salvo G said. "We wish you peace,

brother, and may the devils in your heart be driven out." He turned and marched off in long strides, his flock flowing after.

Bodo waited until they were gone and the morning was quiet again, and then he walked over to where his bike was leaning against a tree. He wound down out of the park and got on The Great Highway. He took the coast road all the way to Los Angeles.

* * *

L.A. was madness. He darted in and out of the smog and the swarming freeway traffic on his battered Honda. He'd never seen anything like it in his life. He wanted to find Bruce King, the astrologer. He wanted to ask Bruce what he was up to. He wanted to ask him to reconsider. Bodo had been spending entire days at the Main Library behind City Hall in San Francisco, and one of the things he'd noticed in his reading was a lack of sincerity on the part of America's spiritual leaders. This lack of sincerity cut through all strata. He'd settled on Bruce King on a whim, as he did everything anymore, trusting the forces inside him. He wanted to ask Bruce about the items he manufactured. His Fast Luck Powder, his Jinx Removing Spray, his ouija board, crystal ball and gold-plated St. Christopher medals. His Star of David, Egyptian scarabaei and holy crosses. He wanted to hear an explanation for all this. He wanted to give Bruce some inside information he'd obviously failed to glean from the stars about the Year One, the danger of mirrors, the salubrious effects of Sun, Fun and Kids and the detriment involved in using certain negative words, how with a little ingenuity these words can be converted into good energy. Bodo had begun laboriously eliminating negatives from his speech.

He drove for hours trying to find the heart of the city. No luck. It seemed the city had no heart. It was a thrashing monster with no central control. He got off the freeway and drove into a shopping mall. He stepped into a glass phone booth and began thumbing through the massive book. There was an army of Bruce Kings. He looked under astrologers in the Yellow Pages and there was no one. He dialed information. No such listing. Bruce had an unlisted number. But Bodo would get through to him, because he had a message. They were all in this together, servants of the same Force. Bodo dialed Sydney Omarr to ask where Bruce could be found.

"I'm sorry, sir, but Mr. Omarr is not in at present. Could I take a message and have him call you back? If it concerns having your chart done, I can quote you a price over the phone. All you need do is mail in the data and a check and Mr. Omarr will return your completed chart within a week."

"No, no! This is *important*! This is Beau Bodo here!"

Silence on the other end.

"Listen, it's very important that I get in touch with Bruce King. Can you give me his number?"

"I'm sorry sir, but Mr. King does not live in Los Angeles. Mr. King is based in New York City. Would you like his address?"

"New York City?"

"Yes sir. If you'd like his address I'll be glad to give it to you, but make up your mind — I have several clients in the office at present."

Bodo placed the receiver quietly back in its cradle. He walked out into the hot day. He unzipped the sheepskin jacket and fanned the two halves back and forth. He hadn't realized how unbearably hot it was. Perspiration trickled down his body. He wiped his face with the back of his hand and looked at it. Rivulets of dirt ran down his hand. Pink areas of skin showed through where the sweat had washed away the dirt.

He sat down on the curb. His bike was leaning against the phone booth. He needed a rest. Perhaps he'd take his bag and throw it on that luscious, isolated patch of grass under that frail lemon tree. No, no. Get back. Back up north. He'd strayed too far. He'd drifted into the epicenter of sin and madness. He got up from the curb and pushed the bike out onto the blacktop. He had no money but he needed gas. He kick-started the bike and idled up to the Texaco station at the far end of the mall. "Fill 'er up," he said.

It didn't make the station attendant happy, Bodo not having any money. He began to swear.

"The Year One is where it's at!" Bodo said. "Sun, Fun and *Kids!*"

The man shook his head. "Get the fuck out of here, buddy, before I call the cops," he said. "Goddamn freaks."

"We're all getting younger!" Bodo told him. Then he started the bike and drove off.

* * *

Now, in Santa Barbara, Bodo was about to gas up again. "Sun, Fun and *Kids!*" he said.

"Fill 'er up?" the attendant said. He was an old black.

"Fill 'er up," said Bodo.

The attendant put the nozzle in the tank and began running in the gas. "My, my," he said. "Looks like you been in a hail storm with this machine!"

"Did it myself!" Bodo said. "To keep it from getting stolen."

The man kept smiling and filling the tank, shaking his head in a mixture of understanding and not understanding.

"I don't have any money," Bodo said.

"Hmm," the attendant said. He did not stop filling the tank. "You don't look like no millionaire, that's for sure," he said.

The pump cut off when the tank was full. "Well, I hope you get to where you're going," the attendant said. "I'll donate this little bit of gas."

"We're all getting younger!" Bodo said.

"I don't know about that," the attendant said, "but good luck."

"Possessions don't have any meaning," Bodo said.

The man shook his head patiently, still smiling.

"Would you like my bike?" Bodo asked.

The man looked into Bodo's eyes, alert. "No, I don't have no use for no motorcycle."

"Take it!" Bodo said, holding out the key.

"No, you just drive off now, I got customers linin' up behind you."

"Okay!" Bodo said. He placed the key on the battered tank, untied his bag, and walked away.

The attendant watched him until he rounded the corner. The people in line began blowing their horns, and he took the bike, which had been leaning against the trash barrel by the air and water hoses, and rolled it into the garage. He returned in a shuffling run to the pumps where the customers had begun serving themselves.

He walked the streets of Santa Barbara with his sleeping bag slung over his shoulder, angling toward the ocean. He knocked on a few doors and announced that he was hungry, leaving the people of Santa Barbara speechless. The doors slammed in his face. The heat was unbearable. He was suffocating in his heavy clothes, fully aware for the first time of their filth, his own stench. He saw only one salvation now — a cleansing.

The beach was empty. He ignored the *Private Property* signs and went straight across the sand, peeling off clothing as he went. When he had stripped to the waist, he sat down and removed his jungle boots and socks. Then he stripped off his jeans on the run, hopping from foot to foot. He'd stopped wearing underwear long ago. He hit the water at a full run, went in about knee deep, and dove.

He was a good swimmer. He could swim forever. Lean, hard Bodo Steiner, his back a map of some journey he could not recall. He surfaced, the salt stinging his eyes. He swam far out from the land, floating on his back, squirted water between his teeth a few meager inches up toward the sky. Closed his eyes and let the sun shine upon him. Ran a hand lazily over his genitals.

Back on shore, he ran along the firm, wet sand where the surf broke. He ran until he was dry and then he walked in toward shore and lay face down in the sand, his head turned to one side and resting on his arm. He slept a rare and dreamless sleep, and his face became that of a small child once again.

One of them put his boot down between Bodo's shoulder blades and yanked his head back by the hair, and the other twisted his hands behind his back and snapped on the cuffs. They pulled him upright and threw his jeans in the sand at his feet. "Put 'em on," they told him.

He stood naked, blinking into the sun. He did not know where he was. He did not know who he was. He tried to bring his hands around to cover his nakedness, but they would not move. They had somehow become webbed together behind his back. The parts of his body were fusing.

"I said put those goddamn pants on! You hear me?" the first cop said. "What's the matter with you? You can't hear? Put 'em on, goddamn it!"

"What's your name?" the second cop said.

Bodo looked from one to the other.

"Don't you know your name? Jack? Henry? Bill? What is it?"

One of them shoved him. He fell back onto the sand, his arms pinned behind him. He lay with his back against the hot sand. He would not tell. Never.

"Jesus Christ, we gotta put your pants on for you?"

"Who needs pants?" Bodo said. "Why don't you take yours off? Sun, Fun and *Kids!*"

The two cops looked at each other and shook their heads. It was an awkward situation. They had carried Bodo's jeans between diligent fingers to where he lay. They had not wanted to touch his filthy pants. They did not want to compromise their manhood by putting on another man's pants for him. They were on a wide-open beach in plain view of the beach-front cottages. They knew that the people in the cottages were watching to see what they would do. Some of them, like the old woman who had phoned in the complaint, had binoculars with which they looked out over the ocean in search of God only knows what. A speck on the horizon. A ray of hope. They had those binoculars trained on them now, while they stood over the naked man. If they beat him, it would not look so good. If they helped him on with his pants, how would that look? They would have to take their chances and uncuff him.

They took off the cuffs and Bodo slid his legs down into his jeans. They yanked him to his feet and cuffed his hands behind him again. They prodded him with their nightsticks toward the patrol car on the road just beyond the beach. They reluctantly gathered the rest of his clothes as they went.

For three days Bodo lay on his cot in the cell. In the mornings they brought him coffee in a tin cup with one piece of dry toast and a restaurant-size box of corn flakes in watered-down milk. In the late afternoon they brought him two bologna sandwiches. At dusk the overhead naked bulb came on automatically, and at dawn it went out. The guard furnished him two packs of Camels and he chain-smoked them into ash.

Bodo smoked them up and spent long hours examining the packaging, the pyramids and palm trees and the camel itself. He thought about the Tigris-Euphrates. His head began to swim with new theories and he disappeared into Egypt while outside the genteel Santa Barbara traffic purred along under a California sun.

On the fourth day he was led from his cell into a small room. The room had no window to the outside. It had wall-to-wall carpeting. It had one table and two chairs. The chair on the far side of the table was a cushioned swivel chair, and the chair on the near side was a straight-back construction of plastic and lightweight hollow tubing. In the swivel chair sat a man about Bodo's age, nearing thirty. He was smiling. He was dressed casually in slacks and a sports shirt. "Hi," he said. "I'm William Blake. Won't you sit down?"

Bodo cocked his head.

"Yes, I know," said William Blake. "What a name. But please sit down and let's get started." Bodo sat down.

William Blake smiled. "They tell me you've been doing a little skinny-dipping," he said.

"Went swimming okay," Bodo said.

"Did you know you were on a private beach?"

"A private beach?" Bodo said.

"Yes. Did you see the signs?"

"Signs and symbols," Bodo said.

William Blake smiled again. "Well, you upset a few old ladies by what you did. Why did you do it?"

"To get clean. And cool. To feel good. I felt bad. I was walking around in all that heat in dirty clothes with a sheepskin jacket on. It was bad. I'd been in L.A. Sin City. Los Angeles has no center, it's a big thrashing monster with no center. I have to get back to San Francisco."

"Oh? They told me you didn't have any I.D. That you wouldn't tell them your name."

"No I.D.?" Bodo held up his arms, turned his hands around slowly in front of William Blake's eyes, tapped his feet on the floor for his ears to hear, wiggled his body. "This is my I.D.," he said.

"Oh, come on. You know what I mean. You know what kind of I.D. I'm talking about."

"Code numbers."

"Just your name would be fine."

"That's a code number too! I give you my name, you have it all. A series of numbers that tell you you know who I am."

"I don't want to hassle you. I want to help get you out of here. Maybe you don't realize it, but you're up against some nasty charges."

"Charges?"

"Right. Charges."

"Like what?"

"Like sexual perversion."

"Sexual perversion?"

"That's right. This is Santa Barbara, not San Francisco. So why don't you tell me your name? I told you mine. Has anyone else in here done that?"

"No."

"Well?"

"Well what?"

"Your name."

"Bodo."

"Bodo?"

"Bodo Steiner."

William Blake sat back in his chair and studied Bodo Steiner.

"You don't believe me," Bodo said.

"What kind of name is that — *Bodo?*"

"German."

"You're from Germany?"

"Why don't you run down my numbers now, they'll tell you the whole story."

"You want to be a smart ass?" William Blake said. "Fine, go right ahead. But you're not in here for a traffic ticket or a DWI, you know. You're in here for indecent exposure. Perversion. For things like that they put the dead data you're talking about aside and go for the throat. That's why you're talking to me now. What they want is your Scout's Honor never to do it again. So don't give me any more shit, okay? Just answer my questions and I'll try to get you out of here. But if you give me a lot of shit, I'll put you through some hoops you never dreamed of."

William Blake took some forms from a satchel he had beside him on the rug. Reading upside down, Bodo made out the words *Wechsler Adult Intelligence Scale.*

"Okay, Bodo. Just answer my questions as truthfully and as simply as possible, alright?"

"Sure."

"What do you mean by Sun, Fun and Kids?"

"It's the San Francisco Kingdom. What isn't Sun, Fun and Kids isn't worth bothering with. It's triadic. The eternal constant. You don't have to *remember* it. It's just there."

William Blake cleared his throat and settled back in his chair. He'd started with an off-the-wall question of his own and got more than he'd bargained for. The test was supposed to take an hour, but a few more questions like that might lead into something that would keep him tied up all day, and it was too beautiful out for that, William Blake had other things to do. He'd stick to the bare bones, and wrap it up fast.

"Bodo, what do you see there?" William Blake pointed to the brown wall.

"A wall," Bodo said.

"And Bodo, what would happen if you tried to walk through the wall?"

"It depends."

"Oh?"

"Depends on the metabolic rate of my brain at the time," Bodo said.

"Do you think it's possible to walk through walls?"

"Sure, people do it all the time."

"All the time?"

"It's been done."

"Really?"

"Yogis do it."

"Can *you* do it?"

"Maybe."

"*Have* you done it?"

"No."

William Blake made a notation.

In spite of his efforts to speed through the litany of the test, the questioning went on longer than William Blake had intended. Bodo gave fascinating answers. He was a good prognosis. He was interesting. In his own peculiar way, articulate. So many who came for help were dumbfounded. They had no idea what was bothering them. They were pathetic and would stammer and stutter and sometimes break down into sobs. Such patients were almost invariably poor and sent off to state institutions or group therapy centers, the Referral Jungle where they were passed from hand to hand.

Bodo was interesting but too poor to bother with. Of course there was the sex angle — Bodo was a handsome boy. Hard and bronze-skinned, tousled blond hair bleached by the sun . . . ah, William — no, no, *no!* A few more questions, and let him go.

"Bodo, you know why you're here, don't you?"

"Sure. I'm a sexual pervert."

"I wouldn't joke about it."

"Who's joking?"

William Blake was suddenly on his guard. Was Bodo coming on to him? Across the table, Bodo had an unnerving grin on his face.

"Do you know what the woman who phoned in on you said?"

"No."

"She said you were floating on your back masturbating."

Bodo shook his head and looked down. Out of nowhere, the weariness came crashing down on him, and he felt the tension in him sag under its weight.

William Blake leaned forward. "Were you?" he asked. He resisted the urge to reach out and lay a hand on Bodo's arm.

"No," Bodo said, still shaking his head and looking at the floor. "I just went to swim. All I wanted to do . . . I just want to get back to San Francisco."

William Blake leaned back in his chair again. His chair creaked like the deck of a ship and they both heard the creaking and in their minds there was the image of a ship at sea, the sensation of that particular peace. William Blake felt a sudden kinship with Bodo. He'd see that he got back home. It would be his good deed for the day.

"Okay, Bodo," he said, and now he did reach out and touch his arm, but it was a different kind of touch. "I'll get you back," he said, and pushed a button concealed under the table.

* * *

He turned the key and walked inside. The landlord hadn't changed the lock, but everything else had changed. The walls had been painted over and the windows had been washed inside and out. The drapery had been replaced. The parquet floors had been refinished and all traces of Bodo's presence had been wiped out. He walked through the empty rooms, smelling new paint and varnish. He went into the bathroom; the porcelain sparkled. He stood in front of the mirror and for the first time in months saw the face of what he had become.

Outside night slipped over the city, and the fog tumbled silently in from the ocean. He left the apartment, walked down to Oak Street, and stuck out his thumb.

* * *

When he got to Reno he was given a job sweeping up in one of the lesser casinos. He received meals and a place to sleep in a custodial shed in the alley. And then Sunday rolled around and he did it.

He stood in the vestibule of the church and listened to the sermon. It was a sermon tailor-made for Reno. The good father was doing his best to reconcile the teachings of Christ with the gambler's lust. It was a noon Mass and filled to capacity. When the priest had finished his sermon, which was mercifully short, he faded back into the ancient ritual of the Church and set about the business of turning bread and wine into the flesh and blood of Christ. He elevated the host and the altar boy rang the chimes. The gamblers were on their knees with their heads bowed. The women among them had hats on their heads and perfume on their bodies. The men had their hair slicked back and wore shaving lotion. They all had sweat in their armpits and the church was heavy with scents.

Bodo came up the center aisle on all fours. "God is Dog!" he exclaimed. "And Dog is God. We're all going back to the Year One! Sun, Fun and *Kids!*" And he began to bark like a dog.

He reached the front of the church and came to his feet. It was cold outside, and he was barefoot. He was dressed in jeans and a filthy T-shirt. His eyes were on fire with zeal. He stood eye-to-eye with the priest, barking at him, and the priest laid down the body and blood of Christ and made for the phone.

Bodo turned and faced the congregation. Most of them were still on their knees, but some of the men had come to their feet. Before they could act, Bodo dropped to all fours again and went barking back down the aisle, out the door and down the steps of the church.

They found him in the men's room of a gas station, sitting on the john with his pants up, his hands folded in his lap. He gave no resistance, but they roughed him up getting him to the car anyway, delivering short, swift punches and chops to those vulnerable places on the body their training had taught them about. They drove him downtown with their siren wailing and their red and blue lights flashing. He lay on the back seat, his hands cuffed behind him once again, staring at the floor, at the flecks of tinfoil from cigarette wrappers, the dry blood stains and particles of dirt and sand. The entire back seat was caged in a mesh of steel.

The shock of what he had done was hammering him further back into himself. He felt as though he was falling down a deep, flesh-like tunnel, the brilliant white light at the opening of the tunnel growing smaller and smaller as he fell away from it.

The moment they had him in a cell, their anger disappeared. They were all part of the same system now. Bodo paced the cell, preaching to them. Their punches and blows hadn't slowed him down a bit. They admired him for this. So many of the tough ones curled up like babies at their feet, but not Bodo. "Sun, Fun and *Kids!*" he told them. Already it had become as familiar as a TV commercial to them. It would repeat itself in their minds over and over again as they drove home after a shift at the station, as they kissed their wives in the kitchen of their split-level homes, as they took their children into their arms and kissed them into sleep at night.

The Year One! — that would stick, too. Almost everything the madman pacing the cell said stuck in their heads. It made no sense, but it stuck. They brought the desk sergeant down to witness their prize and he went and got the lieutenant and two plainclothes narcotics detectives.

"What do you think he's on?" they asked the narcs.

"I don't know," the narcs said. "It's hard to say. It could be anything."

All that day he paced his cell and called out his slogans, and eventually other prisoners down the tier, in an effort to silence him, began calling things back and banging things around between their cell bars. Two days later, when they finally came for him, he was still at it.

They took him down the hallway in cuffs with a guard on either side and led him into a room for questioning.

"Yes, I can walk through walls," Bodo said before the man on the other side of the table could speak. "I can fly through the *sky* too. Sun, Fun and *Kids!*"

"Take him to the hospital," said the man on the other side of the table. "Give him treatment."

* * *

The nurse and two orderlies at the main desk set about doing their job. They took his belongings and listed them. They put the belongings in a wire basket and filed it under "S."

"Follow me," one of the orderlies said. He opened a door and turned to see if Bodo would follow. The other orderly remained leaning against the wall.

They went down a long corridor with no natural light. The light came from bulbs on the ceiling. The bulbs were spaced so that the distance between them graduated from brightness into dimness and then back into brightness again. At the end of the corridor the orderly opened a heavy metal door with a key and they continued down another corridor that went off at a right angle. This corridor, also, was without natural light.

At the end of the second corridor they came to another metal door that opened with a key onto a room that was empty except for a wooden bench, hooks on the wall over the bench, and a tiled area with chrome shower heads and faucet knobs sticking out of the wall.

"Take your clothes off," the orderly told Bodo.

Bodo did not want to take his clothes off, and another orderly came in through a door Bodo hadn't noticed.

"Please take your clothes off and shower," the new orderly said.

"Sun, Fun and Kids!" Bodo said. "Let's *all* take a shower!"

The orderlies exchanged looks. The smaller of the two, the one who had led Bodo down the corridors, turned and left the way he'd come in. The other leaned up against the wall with his arms folded, smiling.

Bodo began explaining to him how the world was formed and what shape it would eventually assume. The orderly continued smiling. Then the smaller man returned with a nurse who carried a syringe on a chrome tray.

They wrestled Bodo to the floor. They pulled his pants down around his ankles and the nurse gave him the injection. Bodo resisted a moment longer, and then he felt himself being ripped away from everything that was his. He was floating above himself. He was detached. Something inside him strained to reunite with his body, but it was no use. He could not get back into himself.

They picked his body up and took off its clothes. They led the body to the shower, placed it under a nozzle and turned on the water. They put a bar of soap in the body's hand and told it to wash. It began randomly moving the soap over its parts.

Then they beckoned the body out of the stream of water and had it sit down on a metal stool. They lathered its head with the bar of soap. They sent it back under the stream of water and then they took it and dried it. The nurse watched. The orderlies had gotten very wet and would have to change uniforms. They dried Bodo roughly. They were not happy with him. The nurse said something to the orderlies and then left. After she had gone, the smaller of the two orderlies took the towel they had been drying Bodo with and snapped it at his genitals.

Bodo's hands came around in slow motion to offer protection, but the towel snapped again, and a message of pain reached the brain from the body far below. Tears came to the eyes and the head shook a mild admonishment, but again the towel snapped, and the orderlies laughed.

"Little fucker," the small orderly said. "We'll teach you to come in here acting like God Almighty. We'll teach you a thing or two before we're done."

Then they dressed him in green pajamas and put an orange bathrobe on him. The bathrobe had no buttons or cord to tie it closed. They put a pair of slippers on his feet, cotton with elastic on the sides, made to fit anyone.

Bodo lay in bed. All around him there was the sound of heavy breathing. He was in a line of identical beds. From a hallway, through an open door, came light. The light came straight to his eyes and gathered there. The light made his eyes want to close, but he forced them to stay open. He fought sleep.

He was clean. He was immaculate. He could not smell himself. For weeks on end he had lived with the smell of himself, and now it was gone. There were no familiar smells anywhere. The sheet on which he lay pulled loose and slid around on the plastic mattress cover. The wool fiber of the blanket over him prickled his skin through the thin covering sheet and his pajamas. He turned his head away from the light without closing his eyes and tried to think, tried to get his body and mind together again. He fell asleep.

It was still dark when an orderly stuck his head into the room. "Okay, let's go, everyone up!" he said in a loud, stern voice, and disappeared again.

Bodo opened his eyes. He was staring into the eyes of the man in the bed to his left. The man stared for a moment and then rolled away to the far side of his bed, pulling the covers over his head. Bodo sat up and looked around him. There were five other men in the room, and they had all pulled the covers over their heads.

The orderly returned and made them all get up. They made their beds and placed identical bedspreads on them. Then they shuffled out into the Day Room in their slippers. The TV was already going, and a meteorologist was speaking of highs and lows.

Other men were already in the Day Room, some of them settled in front of the TV or thumbing through dated magazines, others playing cards, and some simply sitting with their legs stretched in front of them, their hands crammed into their robe pockets. The first light was in the sky, and Bodo went to stand in front of the window, waiting for the sun. There were no bars, and as the sun rose and the grounds became visible, he saw that there were also no walls. Then two orderlies came into the Day Room pushing a cart, and the men began lining up. The orderlies administered medication to the patients along with tiny paper cups half-filled with clear water. When they were done, they came over to Bodo by the window.

"Hi, new guy," one orderly said in a friendly voice.

"The sun," Bodo said, pointing out the window.

"Your medication," the orderly said, and held out a hand with two small pills nestled in its palm.

Each morning after medication, the men went to the dining area and ate their breakfast. Orderlies leaned against the walls, their arms folded across their chests. Bodo forced himself to think. They always lean against the walls, he observed. They always lean that way with their arms folded. All of them. If they don't have something to do, if there's even a minute and a half without direction, they go over and lean against the wall. And then he would lose the thought and begin toying with his food.

Sometimes in the dining room things would go amiss. A patient would disregard his silverware and begin eating everything with his hands — meat, mashed potatoes — everything. Usually this was handled easily enough by an orderly: "Now just look at yourself, Mr. Jones, look what a mess you're making in front of all your friends. Aren't you ashamed?" And Mr. Jones would hang his head and allow himself to be led from the room, sometimes weeping.

But other times dipping his fingers down into warm potatoes and gravy gave rise to a peculiar excitement in a patient, and before you knew it he would be scooping up handfuls of the stuff and slapping it down on top of his head, his face lit with joy, cooing and gurgling noises working up out of him. When this happened, unless the orderlies came off the walls and acted fast, a contagion set in and everyone began slapping mashed potatoes and gravy around.

The dining room was the place where things were most apt to go wrong. There was something about food that could trigger rebellion in the most docile patients. The food was kept as bland as possible, but still things happened, and for the orderlies, it was the most trying part of the day.

The entire day was routine. After breakfast the men did menial chores — mopping, dusting, window washing. Then they were free to sit in the Day Room or go out on the grounds. If they went out on the grounds, they could mingle with the women from the other wards. They could sit in the swings or go down the slide. Follow the dirt paths around and around through the rock gardens. Visit the small canteen where visitors sometimes waited.

But no one went outside. Their medication kept them anchored to the Day Room where they watched TV and stared at magazines. There was a pool table in the Day Room, and occasionally someone would go over and knock a few balls around. And there was a ping-pong table, too.

Bodo came back from breakfast on his first day and sat down heavily in a comfortable chair by the window. He watched the day come and go. Before lunch they gave him more medication. Before bed, more again. He sank into sleep. By the third day he had stopped trying to unite his mind with his body. A flicker of warning passed through him. His theories and slogans turned a watery pink in the channels of his brain. He dug down deep and found a hidden strength. The next time they gave him his medication, he worked the pills under his upper gum and swallowed the water. He went to the bathroom and spat the pills into the toilet. They bobbed around, their flamboyant colors contrasted against the white porcelain bowl. He flushed them down.

He'd been there a week and no one talked to him. No one had analyzed him or categorized him. His file lay on the director's desk. The director had to decide what should be done with the man who barked at God, but the director was not there. He was off fly-fishing.

Bodo was becoming a nuisance. He was rippling the routine with his incessant questions. He was awfully hyper for a man juiced on Stelazine.

"Sun, Fun and *Kids!*" he sang out to the other patients.

They gave him rueful smiles or negative shakes of the head or blank stares.

"Not like that! Like this!" he'd tell them, and shake his head up and down in a positive way.

He would take vigorous walks on the dirt paths. Pump the swing so high it threatened to go over the top. And the other patients gathered at the Day Room window and watched him swing. Watched him go down the slide. Watched him do a little dance for them on the green grass. Watched until they grew restless and began to pace about. Their medication was increased, and they settled back down, faded back from the window.

It didn't take them long to figure out what Bodo was doing. He wasn't the first. They caught him flushing the pills away, and then they took him into a padded room, held him down, and slapped a syringe of Stelazine into his rump. They kept him in there for three days. They brought him food blended into a paste and forced it down his throat. His thoughts leveled out into a white line. In his head there was the image of a white line humming through an infinite, colorless space. White motion on white stillness. He anchored himself on the nuance. Then the drug would wear off a bit, the white line would begin to shimmer like a heat wave, and he would try to get to his feet. But he had no sense of balance and would only crash about like a large beast with a bullet in its heart. That's why the room was padded, to protect him from himself. When they heard him thumping off the walls, they would go in and pacify him.

At midnight of the third day, they took him in a wheelchair to the showers. Two orderlies stripped him of his soiled pajamas and washed him. They put him to bed and he slept the next day away. The day after that he was taken to the director who was back from vacation.

"Tell me, Bodo, what does it mean, Sun, Fun and Kids?"

The thin white line had broken up into a heavy mist that lay over his mind. Above the mist, he could feel the sun's heat. The sun was trying to break through. He sat shivering in his pajamas and bathrobe on the other side of the desk from the director, waiting for the sun's heat to reach him. He ached all over and was deadly tired.

"Bodo? Did you hear my question?"

"The sun is trying to reach me," Bodo said. "To warm me."

"I see," the director said. "Where are you cold? Where do you need the sun's warmth?"

"The sun is good. The sun is primary. Primary numbers are the key to all goodness."

"And what is bad?"

Bodo shook his head. The pain of concentration was overwhelming him. "Dab," he said. Then, his mind making its first wild association in days: "*Brylcreem!* A little dab will do ya!"

The director smiled. "Yes, yes. But you didn't answer —"

"Dab!" Bodo said. "Dab, dab, *dab!*"

The director frowned. Bodo had leaned forward in his chair, jabbing the air with his finger on each *dab*. "Dab, dab, *dab!*" he'd said, jerking the words out as if shooting a pistol in the director's face. The director made a notation.

"Bodo," the director went on, leaving the topic of Sun, Fun and Kids, "what do you understand by the Year One?"

"We're all going back!" Bodo said. "Back to the Year One!"

"Where is the Year One?" the director asked.

Bodo stared at him. "You'll see," he said flatly. "You'll see."

The director and Bodo had three one-hour sessions together on three successive days. In that time the director discovered that nowhere in Bodo's language could negatives be found. He discovered that it would be all peaches and cream when we reached the Year One. He discovered that Bodo was not facing up, that he was constructing an alternative reality into which he was rapidly moving — lock, stock and barrel. He was living in a fantasy world. He was paranoid and schizophrenic. He suffered from primary narcissism and was a manic-depressive. He was a mess. He thought all things were an extension of himself and he was trying to break down the social patterns he'd been born into in order to get back to raw perception. He was trying to liberate himself from all restraints.

Back on the ward, Bodo again began flushing his medication away. But he kept a low profile. He lay awake all night staring at the light on the ceiling in the hallway outside the open ward door, his mind frantic with patterns of thought that grew constantly more sophisticated. He lay quietly and watched the thoughts evolve.

For the first week after the sessions with the director, he followed the routine carefully, and then, while sitting in front of the Day Room window one day, looking out over the grounds and across the desert, a thin incision was made in the fabric of his thought. He turned abruptly in his chair. There was nothing there, only two patients with their robes flapping as they swung green paddles to make contact with the small white ball. Tick-tock . . . tick-tock . . . tick-tock was the sound the ball made as it was shuffled back and forth between the paddles, and it lifted Bodo from his chair and out onto the grounds.

He sat quietly on a swing and felt their eyes on him as they looked down from the Day Room. They were smiling. They were waving. They were calling his name. "Hey Bud!" they called. "Hey Bud, wanna go for a ride in the jeep? Come on, Bud, let's take a dip in the lake! Shake a leg now!"

Bodo closed his eyes and his hands gripped the warm knotted links of the swing's chain and in his mind swirled a galaxy of memory and fantasy. When he opened his eyes again they were filled with tears and he saw two orderlies approaching him across the slope of grass. As soon as they laid hands on him, he began screaming.

He spent a week on a locked ward laid low with Serentil. Then they brought him back to the regular ward and within three days he had convinced half the patients to flush away their medication. Suddenly the men were wandering about the hospital, making contact with the women's ward, and one day a nurse looked out the window to see a man and a woman on the teeter-totter. There were other men and women out there, a few sitting quietly in the swings, and one well geriatric feebly pushing the merry-go-round, trying to get up enough speed for a ride. They moved about as if in a dream, tentative and still unsure of themselves.

Everyone was brought back inside and medicated, and that was the end of that. Bodo was taken to the director where he got into a heated argument and had to be removed by staff. They gave him Electro-convulsive Therapy every day for a week, and then he was quiet. For the rest of the summer he wandered around the ward, occasionally straying out onto the grounds, but always coming back without any trouble when they went out to get him. Gradually he blended in with the rest of the patients and was no longer given special attention, and then one morning his bed was empty when the orderly stuck his head in the door and yelled the men awake. The director issued a routine notification to the highway patrol and the police in Reno.

At the station in Reno, the desk sergeant remembered the name. "Hey, Garrison," he said. "Remember that one guy, that kook who was barking in the church?"

"Yeah," Garrison said. "I remember. Sun, Fun and Kids, right?"

"Yeah. He's loose. He walked off the Funny Farm."

"Yeah?"

"Yeah."

"Think he'll come back here?"

"I don't know. What else? He'll never make it very far on the highways."

"Maybe he'll get a good ride."

"I doubt it."

"Why?"

"Why? Listen, who's gonna pick up a guy who barks at God?"

 V: The Dream

He stood along the wall a few doors down from the Coffee Gallery with his hand out and for a long time said nothing. Then he brought up the words: "Spare change?" But it came out hoarse, and the couple passed by without looking at him. "Spare change?" he repeated over and over, until finally there was the startling sensation of someone's hand touching his, gone as quickly as it came, leaving behind the cool feel of a coin.

He lived near the boiler in the basement of an apartment on Gough Street not too far from North Beach. He was supposed to do odd jobs around the building to earn his keep, but days went by when he was required to do nothing. The old Italian landlady had given him the cot near the boiler out of compassion, and he knew it. He never bothered her. He never told her about the Year One. He seldom spoke of it to anyone. He'd stopped using Sun, Fun and Kids when he found himself drunk on wine one night, standing on the corner of Green and Grant and screaming it at the top of his voice.

He began lying on his cot all day in the dim light of the basement and going out late at night to roam the quiet streets. Sometimes he'd walk the streets until daybreak, and when he returned to the basement, he'd often find slices of sourdough bread and cold leftovers from the landlady's table. He ate this food absently, without gratitude or shame, and then he slept.

One night, lying on his cot in the dark and caught between the loneliness of his solitude in the basement and the loneliness out on the streets, he began talking to himself. His voice had grown deep and coarse and it was foreign to him in the isolation of the dark basement. After a few sentences, he lay silent again, curled up small under his blanket, sensing shapes gliding through the dark. The city of his dreams had been reduced to rubble, and the raging aftermath of fire storms was now dying down. There was the moaning of children hovering about their stricken mothers. Soon the darkness would be complete again, and the real suffering would begin, the real terror, as the children drew together in bands and began to roam.

Fragments from his past lay scattered across the floor of his mind like broken dolls, and he'd pick them up at random, frowning at them; at times he would place them next to each other, prop them up and stand back to study them. Derive meaning from them. Or solace. Anything. He wasn't sure. His own deceptions lay between him and the answers he sought like a vast mine field. And then he heard the voice.

It was well past midnight and he had been talking to himself for hours. He'd been doing it for months, and he no longer feared his own voice or the imaginary shapes that glided through the darkness, brushing against his cot and dissolving again, their raspy breath melding with furnace noises.

"Can you hear me?" the voice said.

At the kitchen table in Beaumont, Sergeant Jansen is arm wrestling with Walter Steiner. Beads of sweat stand out on their foreheads. Their arms are trembling with the strain. They are both dressed in fatigues, combat boots and shoulder-strap

T-shirts. Sergeant Jansen is burly and robust; Walter is ashen and eaten up by cancer; neither man is making headway. Bodo stands watching at a distance. He is only four years old. His body is rigid, his eyes a lucid green, his back a brutal topography. On the other side of the room stands Alma. Bodo and Alma stare into each other's eyes over the table at which the two men struggle. And then Alma begins moving toward them. As she approaches, she begins undoing the buttons of her blouse. Slowly she slips the blouse over her shoulders and lets it fall to the floor in a smooth, silken puddle. She steps out of her skirt and stands at Jansen's side in her full-length slip. Bodo watches as she begins moving against Jansen. Like a snake, Alma moves her body against him. She bends over him and presses his head to her breasts, and Jansen's arm begins to go down.

"*Nein!*" Bodo screams. "*Nein!*" He stands rooted to the spot with his small hands in fists at his sides.

For a moment, just before Walter pins Jansen's arm to the table, Jansen looks over at Bodo and imparts to him one last lesson. Something in his eyes about pain and paradox and how loneliness is only an echo of joy. And then Jansen is gone, as if he had never been there, and they are not in Beaumont but in Germany again, the three of them sitting around the table, Alma reaching over and filling Bodo's glass with milk for the third time. "Trink dat," she says. "It ist gut for hue."

"I said, 'Can you hear me?' "

There it was again. Bodo felt himself surfacing. The people moving about in his mind slowed into rigidity and lifelessness again. The world broke into fragments that froze in place.

"What?" he said into the darkness. "Who's that?"

"I hear you talking all the time."

"Where are you?"

"I live in the room over you. I hear you through the vent."

It was a woman's voice. Bodo lay in the dark and said nothing.

* * *

"Please answer me," the voice said.

He lay on his cot with the blanket thrown back. He was covered with sweat. He was still trembling from the dream. It had been a real dream, not the talking or the trance-like state that he often fell into. It had been a nightmare.

"I know you can hear me," the voice said.

He took a deep breath. "Yes, dear, I hear you," he said.

"You had a bad dream," said the voice.

They'd become acquainted, Bodo and the voice. For weeks they'd been talking through the vent. She'd told him her name, which was Annette, but Bodo persisted in calling her dear.

"Watches," Bodo said. "I was walking through the forest on a cushion of leaves, and suddenly the leaves became watches, millions of them, and I began to sink down into them. I went all the way under and kept sinking. I sank real slow, but it was like there was no bottom to it and I was going to sink forever, and all the time the ticking! All those goddamn watches ticking and ticking and ticking!" His hands lay at his sides, opening and closing into fists.

"It was a bad dream," Annette said.

"Yes, dear," he said.

Sometimes at night he would stand across the street in the shadows and watch the vagueness of her form moving from room to room behind diaphanous curtains. It was impersonal. He would not have recognized her on the street. He did not tell her he did this, but he knew it was alright. He knew the rules. He knew, for instance, that it would have been against the rules to accidentally meet her on the stairs at three in the afternoon, Annette with her arms full of groceries, the TV guide sticking out from the top of a bag, and Bodo with a grease-stained cardboard box full of yesterday's pastries.

It was pastries that he ate more and more. He showed up at five a.m. and stared through the window. When the baker saw him he did not show that he saw him but went to the back room and came out with the box. He opened the front door and placed the box on the sidewalk. After the baker had closed the door and returned to his duties, Bodo picked up the box and took it back to the boiler room. He'd begun fixing up the boiler room. He'd hung an old section of burlap across the doorless entrance and he'd brought in crates that had been discarded by the shops in Chinatown, sturdy boxes with mysterious calligraphy stenciled on their sides. He picked up a lamp and a few dog-eared books from the Salvation Army and placed them on the boxes. He found a throw-rug in a garbage heap and placed it on the concrete near his cot. He got a transistor radio for two dollars and sometimes he would lie in the dark with the radio next to his ear, listening to San Francisco's DJs. At such times Annette would lie in the dark and listen to the music, distorted by the vent, hugging her pillow to her, her eyes closed.

* * *

In the dream he lies in the blue mountain cold in his pajama bottoms and waits to die. He is young enough that he does it with instinct and patience. Then the night grows pale and the sun rims the horizon, low and far to the south. Golden light floods over the snow that stretches and rolls from him in all directions with patches of spring earth already showing through, and billions of tiny snow crystals ignite and sparkle like diamonds. The child locks in on this frigid profusion of beauty and begins making the transition. His eyes close slowly, then open with the same rhythm, but when they do the sky and the dancing light have been blocked out by a face only inches from his, breathing warm air on him. The youth sees that he is alive and straightens up. He turns abruptly and trudges through the snow back into the trees. He returns shortly with two other boys, teenagers with canvas-wrapped rifles slung barrel down. They stand in a circle around the boy and observe him without speaking. The snow into which he has burrowed is crimson with his blood.

"He won't make it," one of the boys says, speaking in the local dialect.

"The Russians will get him, or the cold."

"The Russians have already had him."

"*Ja, ja. So sieht's aus.*"

The third boy says, "We will carry him to the wagon. We will take him with us." He takes off his tattered coat and hands it to one of the other boys. Without any further discussion they carefully bundle the child in the coat and carry him to the wagon. But he is being taken against his will, and he struggles against them until he goes unconscious.

They come down from the higher elevations, and life becomes a cart ride through the aftermath of destruction under a moonless night sky. Daytime is spent lying in ferns and bushes. The intricate world that carries on close to the earth's crust opens up to him. Insects scale the wall of his arm. Spiders come to rest on his knuckles, whispering through their hairy jaws, dancing their spider dance on his flesh. He smiles, and then his eyes lose focus. He has stopped resisting.

As the weeks go by, the remaining bravado drains from the young soldiers, and they become boys again. They have always been boys. By the way they boasted and swaggered, it could be seen that they were only children. There was none of the stealth of purpose in them (back in those heady days of endless victories) that could be seen in the seasoned soldiers, the seasoned citizens who knew what the stakes were, what the consequences of failure would be. And then it happened, and the hounds of hell came baying across the land. Word reached them from the east that in Berlin the Russians had gone amok, raping and laying waste to the city. The boys, the young soldiers, sling their rifles and take to the back roads.

They pass through villages and cities. The cities lie in rubble, bombed out. The villages are braced and awaiting the enemy. They pray for the Americans, but they know about Berlin and fear it will be the Russians. The boys head in a southwesterly direction.

Before reaching Munich, they discard their rifles, fling them into the Isar. They fall in with an endless stream of humanity, pulling their wagon toward the city. All along the way, Americans with German translators are pulling people to the side of the road and questioning them, and some people are taken away in trucks. The boys abandon their wagon and take to the fields. They bring the boy with them.

They enter the city before dawn, moving from doorway to doorway, wending their way through the ruins and the meager first signs of reconstruction. They stumble across the Ludwig Strasse Clubhouse and read the sign that welcomes youth. It's the best they can hope for for the boy who does not speak. They place him in the doorway with a folded coat under his head and a tattered blanket over him. *"Bleib hier, Jünge,"* they tell him, and then they leave.

The boy stares at the cobbled street. He runs his hand over one of the stones, takes in its contours, runs a finger through the miniature ditch that circles and defines it, scans through the light of the greying morning the vast sea of stones that stretches away from him up the empty street. Then he sleeps.

She's almost exactly his age, born on September 29th. "We're both Libras," she tells him. He remains silent. "Do you believe in astrology?" she asks. At times she can ask five or ten or even more questions in a row, and he will not answer. Then she grows sad and they lie in their separate beds without speaking. At such times, she notices, things seem better understood. Slowly she learns about silence, and her questions grow fewer.

He doesn't know when he was born, that's why he doesn't answer. He has an arbitrary birthday. His birthday will be September 23rd, the director at the orphanage decreed. And so it was.

"Do you remember any of what it was like before they brought you to America?" she asks. From their many nights of talking through the vent, she has put together a sketch of Bodo's life, and lately she has been probing him for more information in order to fill out the picture. When Bodo realizes what she is doing, he begins resisting with insolence and mockery.

"Why don't you come down here?" he says. "Are you afraid of the Big Bad Wolf? Are you an ugly girl? Come down here and crawl under my blanket. Do you know what I'm doing right this minute?"

She doesn't answer, and through the silence he can feel her hurt. He clenches and unclenches his fists and feels the tears coming. They come all the time lately, for no reason at all. He'll be leaning into his stride going up a hill for a view of the city, and it starts. Or he'll be hanging around for spare change on upper Grant. Spare change, he'll say, and his eyes fill with tears. So he taunts her. Says obscene things. And in the silence that always follows, he is filled with desolation and doesn't know why he does it.

And then one night, after months of living in the basement, he wakes up from a sound sleep into a state of great clarity.

He lies very still in the dark, and a memory, etched in fine detail, surfaces from deep within his mind. He sees a man larger than life, his great hands lifting Bodo up, high up, higher and higher into the air, the trappings of the world falling away into a black pit of nothingness. And then Bodo is sitting astride those massive shoulders, the man's hand holding him secure by the legs, and they are moving, striding through space, and Bodo is the sun of the universe and the universe is filled with light from corner to corner and everything is equated to joy as Sergeant Jansen strides out of the Ludwig Strasse Clubhouse with Bodo on his shoulders, his arm around the big man's neck, his small hands locked together, hanging on. Life surges through him again, and Jansen grins when he hears the small boy's laughter coming from above him after so many months of silence, and passers-by on the street can not help but smile. Bodo lies on his back in the dark basement, his hands locked behind his head, lost in this vision. He does not hear Annette calling his name.

✳ ✳ ✳

Bodo took the square piece of cloth he'd cut from a large rag and let the water run over it and into the basement utility sink. He stood naked in front of the sink. He had a bar of Ivory soap in one hand and the cloth in the other. He tested the sink one last time, and then he carefully climbed into it, squatting like a yard boy. With an old plastic cup he took water from the running tap and poured it over his head. He did this several times, and then he began rubbing soap into his hair. He poured more water over his head until he'd gotten all the soap out, and then he began washing himself. When he was done, he stepped from the utility sink and stood dripping water on the cold concrete. He took the remainder of the material from which he'd cut his washcloth and dried himself as best he could. He stood by the boiler, moving from foot to foot, his arms crossed in front of him. When he was thoroughly dry, he began dressing in the clean clothes he'd gotten just that morning from the Salvation Army. He combed his hair next, standing in front of the sink again. He had a section of mirror fastened in the pipes that went up along the wall from the sink. In the dim light of the basement, he saw his face as a network of deep shadows and hollows. He brushed his teeth with his index finger and toothpaste, and then he went to the Greyhound station and got a bus down the peninsula.

A month earlier, while sitting over a cup of coffee in a diner, he'd run across this ad in the *Chronicle:* "Ever wanted to be a DJ? Now's your chance! Buy an hour of air time and spin your own records! Be a DJ for an hour over radio L-O-V-E! For details . . . " He went directly to the Chinaman at the Hoosier Stick. The Chinaman would not let him work the floor, but he gave him a job sweeping up in the morning for four dollars a day.

Radio LOVE was situated in a three-story house on a very staid street in a very respectable neighborhood. It was a small 1000-watt station run by a group of liberal-minded college graduates and financed by a rich eccentric from Texas. They broadcasted only the latest, most progressive acid rock — message music. To raise a little money, and out of a sense of community, they hatched the scheme of selling air time to their listeners. For twenty-five dollars an hour, it was possible to walk into Radio LOVE between the hours of midnight and two a.m. and play DJ, sit in the magic seat in front of the console, and blow your own mind just looking at all those knobs and needles. You couldn't touch them, however. You couldn't even cue your own records. You whispered to one of the station personnel what music you wanted to play, and they took care of the rest. What you could do was sit there with your heart in your throat and sputter into the mike: "And now I'd like to play for you . . . Ravi Shankar's latest hit, dedicated to all sentient beings out there in the world of MU, especially Maharishi Mahesh Yogi . . ."

Bodo stood in front of the house and compared its address to the address he'd written on the piece of paper in his hand. They corresponded. He went up the walk and through the door. He found himself on a very thick carpet. In front of him was another door, and on it was a modest sign that read: RADIO LOVE. He opened this door and went in. More carpet. Very dim light. No sense of radio station as he knew it. He went hesitantly down the hallway, and then (down a corridor that led off to his right) he saw the green glow. He went toward it.

The green glow was coming through the soundproof glass of the control room, from the lights on various panels. The DJ was sitting in a tank of eerie green light, talking into his mike in a well-modulated, almost hypnotic voice. Bodo stared at him through the glass. He reached up and tugged uneasily at the tie he'd put on for the occasion. He began shuffling from foot to foot and his mouth was as dry as old newspaper.

The DJ (whose voice Bodo could hear coming over the sound system that was hooked up throughout the house) finally looked up and saw him standing there. He finished his lead-in and then cued the record. He left the control room through a door that opened into an adjacent room. A moment later a door opened down the corridor and the DJ stuck his head out. "Yes?" he said. "Can I help you?" The house was now filled with the music the DJ had chosen to play. An oldie but goodie, he billed it. "Life goes on within you and without you," the Beatles crooned.

"Yes, I'm Bodo Steiner," Bodo said, striding up the corridor toward the DJ. "I bought some air time."

"Right," the DJ said. "Well, come on in here and we'll set you up. Do you have a list of the records you want to play, or do you want to scan our selection?"

"I've got a headful," Bodo said, and stepped into the room where there were two other men besides the DJ, passing a joint around.

He hadn't been smoking grass lately. He hadn't been drinking. He'd been washing in the utility sink and fixing up the boiler room and cleaning up in the morning for the Chinaman. He'd been saving his money and dreaming, not the nightmares, not the talking into the darkness, but old dreams. He dreamed of being a DJ again, he dreamed of happiness, and through the vent, Annette nursed his dreams along. But now he took the joint when they passed it to him and drew in the smoke.

Bodo joined in the small talk and tried to imitate the fey modulations that flecked the speech of Radio LOVE's staff. He tried at the same time to keep his feet from tapping and his body from rocking and he tried to keep from constantly glancing nervously at the control room where the records were filed from ceiling to floor and the console and the turntables were waiting. He tried to hide all the things he'd been and all the things he'd become. He tried not to blow it.

"Man, you came all the way down from the *city?*"

"All the way, man," Bodo said.

"But man, you can't pick up our *signal* in the city, dig? We don't *send* that far."

"Hmmm, yes, well. I read about it in the paper. Come down and play some tunes, it said, and here I am."

They studied him with half-lidded eyes. They expected more.

"And . . . I pick you guys up sometimes when I'm driving around . . . on my bike . . . I pick you up on the way to San Jose."

"On your *bike*, man?"

"Right!"

"You pick us up on your *bike?*"

"I got a radio on my bike. Sure. I got earphones. I listen to you cruising down Highway 101, cutting in and out of traffic, the *wind* blowing in my *face!*" He was feeling the grass. "And I thought to myself, 'Bodo, why don't you spin some music for these people there at radio L.... O.... V.... E!'"

They were listening to him now. "Hmmm," one of them said. "Well, let's get started then. Harry, take him in and show him the ropes, okay?"

"Sure," Harry said. "Let's go, friend."

"Okay, this is the way it works. You sit right here."

Bodo sat down behind the console.

"Let me know what records you want to play and I'll pull them for you. You can play a whole LP or a cut, it doesn't matter, and I'll cue it up. Then I'll give you a signal and you introduce it — talk into that mike right over the machine. Then —"

"Console."

"What?"

"It's a console."

"Right. That's what it is. Anyway —"

"It's a Gatesway, modified. Looks like a good board."

"Hey man — what is this?"

"It's a console! And these are the pots. This one here's your monitor gain control, and this one's master gain, and —"

Harry tapped into a mike to the outside room. "Tom, come in here for a minute. You too, Joel."

They came in.

"This guy knows the board," Harry said.

"Who sent you here?" Joel asked.

"No one," Bodo said. "No one sent me here."

"Where'd you learn the board?"

"I got my *two*," Bodo said. "I had my own show. In New Orleans. I mean in — I was a DJ. I —"

"KSAN send you down here to monkey with us? What's the deal?"

"No deal. Let me spin some music, I'll show you. I'm Beau Bodo! Hey! This is Beau Bodo here, coming to you over KP*MP!* Blowing the moss from your bayou *minds!* Yeah, hey *hey!*"

Meanwhile, the Beatles were still spinning out over live air. "This disc is about out," Harry said. "Why don't the three of you step outside for a moment and I'll get something spinning and then we can iron this out."

"Hey! Nothing to iron!" Bodo said. "I'm Beau Bodo and I can *handle* it!"

"Mr. Steiner, I'm afraid I'm going to have to ask you to leave the control room. If you don't —"

But Bodo has tapped into live air and is on the mike, talking over the music.

"Hey! What say, little children? *Is* Sergeant Pepper still worth his salt? *Are* there still enough lonely hearts to form a band? *Does* life go on within you or anywhere else, once you're 64? *Heavy* questions! *Very* heavy questions! But even heavier — is Little Richard *still* the man he used to be? Let's all of us be the judge of that, cruising through the dream of California, let's bring the man out for a re-in-*spec*-tion! Let's spin us some *real* oldies-but-goodies and see for our*selves!*"

While talking he signaled them to bring him the Little Richard records. They stood staring at him, stoned on the grass. It was a dream. A bad dream. This person had come wandering in off the street and had taken over the station. He was sitting behind the controls like he owned the place. The hard thing, though, was that he was doing a passable job of it. He was going out over live air in a viable form. It wasn't Radio LOVE's style, but it *was* style. He wasn't babbling. If he had been, they would have had no choice — they would have had to tackle him and drag him from the station. But the way it was going, no one would know that anything was seriously wrong, and maybe he'd get his fill in a minute or two and relinquish the controls. Maybe he'd kill the control room mikes once Little Richard was spinning, blowing the eardrums of Radio LOVE's advanced listeners, and then they could jump him. They could jump him and get him the hell out of there. Drag him onto the street and send him off on his Honda with earphones. Pacify the callers — and there would most certainly be callers — and perhaps stay clean with the FCC.

They gave him a stack of Little Richard 45s and an adapter for the turntable. He signaled them out of the control room then, and when they hesitated, he leaned back from the live mike and spoke in a clear whisper: "You try to rush me, I'll scream shit piss and motherfucker right into this live mike. I'll scream bloody murder!"

Reluctantly they backed out of the control room. He waved them to the far side of the outside room, and then he jumped up and ran to the door, locking himself in. He went back to the turntables where Sergeant Pepper was coming to the end of side one.

"*Okay!*" Bodo said into the mike. "Here comes the *man*. So up against the wall of your *mind!* Is this the King of Rock 'n' Roll or *what?*" And he brought in Little Richard with "Gonna Rip It Up," badly cued so that at first it sounded like Little Richard was working his way up from the bottom of a barrel of molasses, then bursting through and disappearing over the air waves at the speed of light with all his savage energy into the early-morning ears of Radio LOVE's listeners. The phones began ringing.

"Listen up!" Bodo was saying, cutting in on Little Richard and "Long Tall Sally." "Listen up here! Contest time! A Honda with earphones to the first caller who can rightly identify the man who coined the term Rock 'n' Roll! Drop those *dimes!*"

And he sat back in his chair, swiveling, rocking, the sweat glistening on his face, his mind ripped loose from its recently established modest mooring, adrift once again in that grey sea of loneliness.

Then he glanced out into the other room and saw that there were only two of them. In the darkened corridor, on the other side of the glass in front of him, he saw a shadow glide by. The shadow went gliding by, and Bodo was left looking at his own weak reflection in the glass, his face tired and lined, no longer hard and angular. It wasn't his face. It wasn't his body. Not anymore. He understood this now. He understood this very well. He looked through the glass again at the two men left in the room, and they were staring at him. It was a look he knew. It was the look Jimmy the DJ had given him that day, coming out of the break room with the cup of coffee in his hand after Bodo had told the citizens of the Golden Triangle that Jerry Lee Lewis had set his balls on fire. The very same look. Nothing had changed since then, really. And the loneliness and despair smashed down on him, crushing the matchstick structure of his recently resuscitated dreams.

"Long Tall Sally" had ended and the needle was stuck in the dead grooves at the end of the record. "Sonofabitch, *play* something!" Tom said out loud in the other room. "Don't just sit there — *play* something! What should we do?!" he asked Joel.

"I don't know," Joel said. "Maybe kick the door down? I don't know. Wait until Harry comes back with Mr. Wyatt. Mr. Wyatt will know what to do."

"Jesus, what if he can't locate him? What if he flew back to Texas this morning like he was thinking of doing? What then?"

"I don't know what then," Joel said.

In the control room, Bodo was still staring at the strange face reflected in the glass. He took a deep breath and ran a hand through his hair. He leaned into the mike and spoke. "No one knows," he said. "Not a living soul knows. It was Alan Freed coined those words back in 1951 at the Cleveland Arena. He couldn't say Rhythm 'n' Blues, because Rhythm 'n' Blues meant nigger music . . ."

Tom slapped both hands to his temples and spun around, unable to face the control room any longer.

" . . . and nigger music was kept separate from white music back then, you see, and what Alan Freed had lined up for this concert that a lot of white kids had bought tickets to was nigger music, and so he coined a phrase, he made up a euphemism right then and there over the air, he called it Rock 'n' Roll . . . rock and roll, lock and load, defoliation is a euphemism for treating plants like niggers . . . she loves you — yeah, yeah, *yeah!*"

He trailed off again. His hands were trembling badly. He saw two shadows glide by on the far side of the glass, and then Harry and a rotund man in a rumpled suit wearing a Stetson and puffing a big cigar entered the room adjacent to the control room. The man with Harry also carried a cane that he continually twirled and tapped against the floor and various objects around him, including people, as if testing their mettle.

Bodo pulled himself together when he saw Mr. Wyatt enter the room. Something about Mr. Wyatt inspired him. "Well," he said into the mike. "That's neither here nor there! Dead plants are a green light switched to caution! And Little Richard Penniman *is* the King of Rock 'n' Roll, the savior of us all, born Christmas Day, *1935,* just one week after Elvis but *eons* before! Born in the Year One and getting younger all the time! Going Tutti Frutti with his gal Lucille! Tell 'em about it, Mr. Penniman!" And he sent "Lucille" out over the air waves.

The three phones at Radio LOVE were ringing off their hooks. Nathaniel Wyatt leaned back against the wall, one boot crossed over the other, and puffed on his cigar. "What are they saying?" he asked.

"Oh, Jesus, Mr. Wyatt, I'm sorry about this, but I told you so. I hate to say it, but I told you something like this might happen if we started letting just anyone come in here after midnight. I —"

"What are they saying, Joel?"

"They want to know what's going on."

"Are they angry?"

"I don't know."

Mr. Wyatt walked over and picked up a ringing phone.

"Hey, man, this is a listener out here. I'm in the middle of a trip, man, and I was counting on Radio LOVE for some good vibes. What's going on? You people trying to gross me out in the middle of a trip? Where you coming from with all this heavy karma, man?"

Mr. Wyatt hung up and picked up another phone.

"Hello. My name is Anne. I think it's very informative, the information your new DJ is giving us. I think it's stimulating, how hot and fast his mind works. I —"

And another.

"Jesus, brother, what is this. Are you people reverting to barbarism? I always thought LOVE was in the front ranks of cosmic awareness, but I don't know after tonight. Listen, I'm not just *anyone*. I have connections. My father has connections. I can get through to the FCC. If you think I can't, why you —"

Nathaniel Wyatt hung up. He went back to leaning against the wall. He studied Bodo who was in high gear now, really cooking.

"Take the phones off the hook," Mr. Wyatt said.

"What?" said Tom.

"The phones, stupid," said Joel. "Take them off their hooks. You heard him." Tom didn't move, and neither did Joel. Their faces were glazed in misery. Harry, who had been quietly sitting in a chair, got up and removed the receivers from their cradles.

"Thank you, Harry," said Mr. Wyatt.

"And do you know," Bodo was saying into the mike, "that when the plane came down with a BOOM! why our man Richard Penniman threw all his *rings* and *things* into the dark waters and gave away his Little Richard riches and turned himself over to *God!* Yaas! God is Dog and Dog is God!"

And he spun "Tutti Frutti" and killed the control room mikes and sat back again, drenched in sweat, his tie pulled loose around his puckered, un-ironed collar, a Salvation Army nightmare come true.

"Beau Bodo," Nathaniel Wyatt said, more to himself than to anyone else in the room.

"What? What was that, Mr. Wyatt?" said Joel.

"Beau Bodo," Mr. Wyatt repeated. "That's Beau Bodo in there. Had a program up in Baton Rouge until a few years back. I used to pick him up regular from Port Arthur. One time I was going to buy him up and make him go big, but he just sort of disappeared."

"You *know* him?" Joel said.

"I know *of* him," Mr. Wyatt said, and then went over and cut the power that kept the station on the air.

"You just put us off the air!" Joel cried out in disbelief.

"I just put *him* off the air," said Nathaniel Wyatt, and then he tapped into the control room with a live mike. "Hey, Beau Bodo, how you been, boy?"

Bodo looked up. Someone was calling his name. Someone in a friendly Texas voice.

"How I been? Hey, little children out there in California Land, it ain't no *fault* of yours, but I'm slippin' and a slidin'!

Right into the sea of memory! I hear a voice calling me! 'How you been, Beau Bodo?' the voice says! How you *been* boy!"

"You still cook," Nathaniel Wyatt said. "Where'd you disappear to? I had plans to come on over to Baton Rouge and offer you some big money. I had plans to take you to the top, boy."

Bodo looked through the glass into the smiling eyes of Nathaniel Wyatt. Nathaniel Wyatt was running things around there. He was running things all over the world. Nathaniel Wyatt and Bodo were having a conversation over the air for all the world to hear, and it didn't seem to bother Nathaniel Wyatt one bit. It was his station and his money and his world, and they were walking all over FCC regulations, but he didn't care one iota. He didn't care as much as Bodo did. Suddenly the tables were turned, and it was Bodo who was on the defensive, Bodo who had something to lose, and he didn't even know what it was.

"Why don't you open that door and come on out here and talk to me? You've gone and got my boys here so antsy they're about to wet their pants. Come on out here and let Harry sit in for you. We got things to talk about."

"Tutti Frutti" had just ended, and there was no music playing. "Just one minute," Bodo said, and he cued up "Jenny Jenny." "Hey!" he said into the dead mike. "Hey out there! Stick this in your pipe and *smoke it!*" He lowered the needle onto the record, spun out of his chair, and unlocked the door. He walked into the other room and approached Nathaniel Wyatt with a smile, his hand extended. Nathaniel Wyatt smiled back while Tom put them back on the air and Harry took over at the console.

"Ladies and gentlemen," Harry was saying into the mike behind the closed control room door. "Ladies and gentlemen, we've been experiencing transmission difficulties . . . please stay with us. This is Radio LOVE, 98.6 on your radio dial. Jupiter's in Mars and all is cool under a full and fecund moon . . . love one another . . ."

When Bodo was in reach, Nathaniel Wyatt, still smiling, swung the cane and caught him across the bridge of the nose. Bodo's hands went to his face, and Nathaniel Wyatt swung the cane again, this time catching him in the stomach. Bodo doubled over. Then the cane came down across the back of Bodo's head, and once he'd hit the floor it came down repeatedly across his back and the backs of his legs.

Tom and Joel pulled Mr. Wyatt off. They got Bodo to his feet and led him outside. They sat him on the curb in front of Radio LOVE. They looked around for the Honda with the earphones, but didn't see it.

"Don't you think we should call the police?" Tom said. "Or an ambulance?"

"No, I don't think we should call anyone," said Nathaniel Wyatt, who had followed them outside. He was breathing heavily from his work with the cane. "This here's Beau Bodo," he said. He bent down behind Bodo where he sat on the curb, hunched over and rocking with his arms locked around his legs. "Ain't that right, boy?" he said, his thick lips almost touching Bodo's ear.

* * *

He eased himself down into the tub of hot water, all the way down until only his head and the tips of his knees were above the water line. He closed his eyes. She massaged the shampoo into his hair, kneeling beside the tub on the tile floor, dark stains on her light-blue blouse where water had splashed.

After being ejected from the station, he had wandered around the peninsula for almost a week. He began telling people about Sun, Fun and Kids again, and about the Year One where they were all headed. He sat along walls in shopping centers or on the sidewalk on El Camino Real and panhandled wine money. Once a group of young Chicanos roughed him up after dark, and then he got arrested in San Mateo. He spent three days in jail before giving them the address of the apartment building on Gough Street, using the girl's name and apartment number. She drove down and picked him up.

He sat against the car door, slumped in the seat. He did not speak to her. Not even when they brought him out of his cell and they saw each other for the first time. "Hello, Bodo," she'd said, but he did not answer.

When they got back to the city, he went straight to the basement, and for several days she heard nothing. Then one night he finally spoke.

"Do you hear me?" he said.

"Yes," she said.

"You're a fat girl," he said. "Why didn't you tell me that?"

She didn't answer.

"I don't like fat girls, dear," he said.

Still she didn't answer, and then she heard him weeping through the vent. "Bodo?" she said. "Will you come up here?'

She washed his hair for an excessively long time, massaging his scalp, and then, using a bowl from the kitchen, she rinsed out the soap, first using water from the bath, and then clean water from the tap. She had him stand in the tub of grey filmy water and with a face cloth and a bar of soap she thoroughly washed his body. He was totally submissive and without shyness.

When she had rinsed him, she had him step out onto a bath mat and she dried him with a large Turkish towel. She dried his body and then rubbed his hair vigorously. She did not comment on his scarred back. She stopped drying suddenly, holding his head between her hands with the towel, the towel draping down between them. She held his head and looked into his eyes. With her eyes she drew together all the force she could from the months of talking through the vent, and she drove this force against the deadness that she sensed in him. Over and over she drove against the deadness, until she felt her tears coming, and she knew then she did not have the strength to save him. She looked away, and when she looked back again, he was smiling. It was a terrible, victorious smile. It was not him smiling.